Mal Moulée by Ella Wheeler Wilcox

Born on November 5th 1850 in Johnstown, Wisconsin, Ella Wheeler was the youngest of four children. She began to write as a child and by the time she graduated was already well known as a poet throughout Wisconsin.

Regarded more as a popular poet than a literary poet her most famous work 'Solitude' reflects on a train journey she made where giving comfort to a distressed fellow traveller she wrote how the others grief imposed itself for a time on her 'Laugh and the world laughs with you, Weep and you weep alone'. It was published in 1883 and was immensely popular.

The following year, 1884, she married Robert Wilcox. They lived for a time in New York before moving to Connecticut. Their only child, a son, died shortly after birth. It was around this time they developed an interest in spiritualism which for Ella would develop further into an interest in the occult. In later years this and works on positive thinking would occupy much of her writing.

Here we publish a novel; Mal Moulee. If you think of Ella solely as a poet this might seem a departure into unknown territory. But if you think of her as a writer it instantly becomes part of her domain.

On Robert's death in 1916 she spent months waiting for word from him from 'the other side' which never came.

In 1918 she published her autobiography The Worlds And I.

Ella died of cancer on October 30th, 1919.

INDEX OF CONTENTS

PREFACE

It is more than two years since the outline of this simple story first suggested itself to me, and since the first chapters were written.

Many times since then, conscious that I possessed no talent as a novelist, I have resolved to abandon the work. Yet an unaccountable and mysterious impulse (which no doubt my severe critics will declare as unfortunate, as unaccountable) compelled me to complete it.

I have attempted no fine descriptions, no rare word-painting, no flights of eloquence. These things lie not within my province. As simply and briefly as possible, I have endeavored to relate such events as occur almost daily in our midst.

In Percy Durand, I have described, and possibly, somewhat idealized, a type of man to be found in any of the cities of America.

In Dolores King, the unfortunate and undesired offspring of a loveless marriage fletrie avant sa naissance.

In Helena Maxon, my ideal of

"The perfect woman, nobly planned To counsel, comfort and command."

In my selection of a title, I could find no suitable English term which would express the meaning I wished to convey in unison with the leading idea in the book. Therefore, I was obliged, not without reluctance, to use a French term.

To avoid many personal inquiries, I would say, in the beginning, that while I have known nearly all the experiences herein related to occur, in actual life, I do not, at the present time, know of any person or persons who answer to the characters I have created.

ELLA WHEELER WILCOX.
Meriden, Ct., December, 1885.

CHAPTER I. TWO GIRLS.

Helena Maxon stood at the window which looked out on the tennis court, weeping softly, when her mother's arm encircled her, and her mother's voice, tremulous with tears unshed, addressed her.

"Lena, darling," she said, "you must control yourself. Madame Scranton will return in a moment, with the young lady who is to be your roommate and companion, during the next year. She is a lovely and charming girl; and I do not want my own sweet darling's face to be utterly disfigured by weeping when her new friend first beholds it. I am certain, my dear daughter, that you will be very happy here, and perfectly content after the first loneliness wears away."

"I can never be happy and contented away from you and Papa!" cried the young lady passionately. "I should feel like a wicked, cruel hearted creature, if I became contented and happy when separated from you. I know I shall die of home-sickness before I have been here one term," and her tears dripped anew.

Mrs. Maxon choked down a lump in her own throat, and forced a smile to her lips.

"You will, I know, try to be happy dear," she continued, "when you realize that the happiness of your parents depends upon your own. We have selected this academy as the most desirable institution in which to place you, and Madame Scranton is a lady in every way suited to guide and direct a young girl's mind. It will be very hard for us to live without you, but we know it is for your good, and you will one day thank us for it. Here comes Madame, and the young lady; dry your eyes, dear child, and greet her pleasantly." And while Lena was bravely striving to stem the upward-welling tide of tears with a very moist bit of cambric, she heard Madame's deep contralto voice following her mother's tremulous soprano tones:

"Miss Maxon, let me present your future companion and I trust, friend. Miss Dolores King, Miss Helena Maxon."

As the two girls looked in each other's eyes and clasped hands, no faintest premonition came to either young heart of the strange and tragic destiny which was to link their future lives.

Helena's first thought was, "What a beautiful creature, a perfect Aphrodite." While Miss King was saying to herself, "Rather a nice little body, and almost pretty if she had not disfigured herself by crying."

An artist might have found the two girls a fine study for opposite effects.

Miss King was nearly twenty; tall, and so slight as to seem almost fragile. Her face was exquisitely beautiful in contour, quite classic in its perfectly-chiseled features, and interesting from its mingled expression of pride and melancholy. In color her hair was a pure, pale shade of yellow, like the underside of a canary bird's wing; her skin that firm, yet delicate white, of the calla lily blossom. Her long heavily-fringed eyes were as darkly blue as the heart of a violet, the flower she best loved. A rare, wonderful face, a face that might become a priceless fortune or a blighting curse to its possessor.

Helena Maxon was full half a head below her new friend in stature, and though three years her junior, her figure was much more voluptuously developed. A round face, a clear brunette complexion, a coil of dark hair that exactly matched the color of her eyes, eyes peculiar, from the fact that at times they seemed veiled with a delicate film, which gave the appearance of one in a trance or somnambulic state, a nose which no phrenologist could classify, which we must therefore call irregular (and which was just now swollen and reddened with much weeping), lips too full for beauty, yet a mouth so luscious in bloom, and so sweet in expression, that the beholder instantly forgave it for being large. This comprises a fair pen picture of Helena Maxon, on that September afternoon as she stood in the stiff and orderly reception room of Madame Scranton's Select Academy for young ladies.

"Miss King will show Miss Maxon to her apartments," said Madame, after the two girls had exchanged greetings. "We will join you there, presently." Then, turning to Mrs. Maxon as soon as the young ladies had left the room, she continued: "I wish to assure you, my dear madame, that your daughter could not have a more desirable companion, in this her first absence from you, than the young person you have just seen. Miss King is quite a rare character; I consider her the most reliable pupil in my charge. I have never known her to disobey a rule during the three years she has been with me. I regret that she remains only another year."

"She is very beautiful," Mrs. Maxon said, musingly; "but her face impresses me as a sad one."

"Her nature is tinged with a seriousness which is almost melancholy," Madame replied. "Her mother died when she was but a few months old:

her father married a second time, and unhappily, I believe: at all events, Dolores has made her home with an uncle, a peculiar and austere man; he has given her every advantage, as he is a man of wealth, but she seems prematurely grave and serious-minded, from her association with him. She is very thoughtful, and of marked originality, and absolutely devoid of the vanity one might naturally expect so beautiful a girl to possess. She is wholly indifferent to admiration, and seems to have none of the sentimental weaknesses of youth. I am sure she can only be an advantage and benefit to your daughter. She is, too, a member of an Orthodox church in good standing."

"I am pleased with what you tell me of this young lady," Mrs. Maxon replied. "I fully realize the great dangers to which parents expose their daughters in sending them from home to boarding-schools: it requires the utmost care and surveillance, to surround them with the right influences. The choice of instructors and companions for a daughter at this critical period of her existence, is a matter of vital importance; and one not sufficiently considered. Many a young girl's mind has been poisoned, and her future warped by injudicious companionship at boarding-school. Too often the most careful instructors are utterly ignorant of their pupil's thoughts and conversation outside the class room."

"Quite true: too true," Madame Scranton assented. "But I endeavor as much as possible to render myself the confidant of my pupils: to lead them to talk to me on all subjects as they would talk with their mothers. Having a limited number of young ladies in my charge, this is possible for me, while it could not be successfully done in a larger establishment."

"And that is the reason why Mr. Maxon and myself decided upon bringing Helena to you," Mrs. Maxon continued. "We were convinced that you would exercise a wise supervision over her character and conduct. She is of a strongly affectionate and emotional nature, full of love for humanity, and belief in her fellow beings. I do not want her affections chilled, nor her confidence checked by worldly counsels, or a premature knowledge of the baseness which exists in the world: let her keep her beautiful faith and loving impulses while she may. Only guard her from being led into folly or imprudence. As I grow older I am more and more convinced that the people who constantly strive to impress the mind of the young with distrust for humanity are the people who are themselves unworthy of trust: or else those who have become embittered by sorrows they have not understood. I believe it possible to keep a nature like Lena's sweet and wholesome forever."

"But there are infinite disappointments and bitter experiences in store for a nature such as you describe," Madame suggested. "That beautiful trust must be rudely shattered."

"Shocked, but not shattered;" corrected Mrs. Maxon. "And I think it better in this life to be often wounded through too great faith in our fellow-beings than to embitter our minds with an early distrust.

"I have tried to impress her with the belief, that whatever pain is sent to her, comes as an ennobling and purifying lesson; not as a punishment. I want her to think of her Creator as a Benefactor; not as an Avenger. Her heart is free now, from all envious or jealous emotions, as a carefully tended flower-bed is free from weeds. But she has never been exposed to the constant friction of association with her own sex: and I tremble when I think what emotions evil influences may implant in that fresh soil.

"I want you to teach her, as I have done, that envy is a vice, and jealousy and unkind criticism are immoralities, certain to destroy the noblest character. We warn our sons from the gaming-table and the wine-cup, with loud voices; but too many of us sit silent while our daughters contract habits of malicious speaking and envious criticism, which are quite as great evils in society to-day, as intemperance or gambling.

"You will forgive my lengthy dissertation, my dear Madame, when you remember how precious the trust placed in your care. And now I must bid her a last farewell and take my departure. Poor child! she has never been separated from me a week in her life. The parting will be very hard for both of us."

"Remember, my sweet child," was Mrs. Maxon's last injunctions to her weeping daughter, "that you are always to make me your first confidant in all things. Hear nothing, say nothing, do nothing, which you cannot tell your mother, who will ever strive to be your best adviser. And now, God's angels guard you, dear, and good-by."

And Mrs. Maxon turned hastily from the clinging arms of her daughter, and hurried away, while Helena threw herself upon the couch in a wild passion of uncontrolled tears.

CHAPTER II. TWO GIRLS AND A DOLL

When Dolores rapped softly at the door an hour later, she was bidden to enter by a low but calm voice; and she found Helena busy in unpacking her trunks, and arranging her wardrobe in closets, drawers and boxes.

"You look tired, Miss Maxon," she said kindly "or rather, Miss Lena, for we must not be formal if we are to be room-mates, must we? so let us begin with Lena and Dolores from the first."

"Dolores," repeated Helena, softly; "Dolores, it is a lovely name, but I never heard it before."

"No, it is not a common name. It means sorrowful, I believe; my mother named me well. And now, may I not assist you in your unpacking? Let me hang up your dresses, the hooks are so high, and I am taller than you."

"Oh, thank you, you are very kind, and I am tired. It always makes me tired and ill to cry, and I look so like a fright, too. I wish I might be improved by tears, like the heroines in novels we read about; but I am not so fortunate as they."

"Have you read many novels?" asked Dolores, as she hung up a neat blue walking suit, secretly wondering if that color could be becoming to her dusky companion.

"Oh, no, not many. Mamma thinks I am too young to read the best novels understandingly, and she does not like to have me read anything for just the story of it. I have read all of Mrs. Whitney's books; they are the sweetest stories in the world for girls to read, mamma says, and I think so, too. They always make me feel braver and better, and more contented. I have read two or three books that made me discontented; the heroines were so wonderfully gifted and so gloriously beautiful that I fairly hated my poor self for days after reading about them."

Dolores smiled.

"That is very odd," she said, "I do not remember to ever have been affected in that way by a book."

Helena cast an admiring glance upon her companion.

"Well, I should not suppose you would be?" she responded, "because you are more beautiful than any heroine I ever read about, and that makes all the difference in the world, you know."

Dolores let a whole arm full of mantles and dresses fall in a heap upon the floor, as she turned and stared at the speaker.

"Are you making sport of me?" she asked, bluntly.

"I, making sport of you? Why, I would not be so rude," cried Helena, the tears starting to her eyes again. "Perhaps I ought not to have spoken so plainly, may be you think 'praise to the face is an open disgrace;' but I do not believe that. If I like anything or anybody, I can not help saying so; and I thought you must know how very beautiful you are, and I spoke of it just as I would speak of the beauty of a flower or a picture. I am sorry if I have annoyed you."

Dolores picked up the scattered garments and began to arrange them in order.

"Well, you are the oddest girl I ever met," she said. "But you have not annoyed me; I am sure it is very sweet of you to say such pretty things to me; only I never knew any girl who talked like that before: girls are usually so hateful, you know."

"Are they?" and there was real grief in Helena's voice. "Oh, I don't like to believe that is true."

"But have not you found them so?"

"No; but you see I have known very few girls. I have lived very quietly at home, and I never even staid all night with a girl in my life, mamma never liked to have me. No doubt I have a great deal to learn, but I always longed for a sister, and I thought girls were very nice indeed."

"I suppose some of them are," Dolores admitted, "but I never cared much for their society myself; as a rule they only think and talk about beaus, and marriage, and silly gossip which does not interest me. But I'm sure you are quite different, and we shall get along nicely together. For pity's sake, what is that!"

This last exclamatory query was uttered just as Helena unfolded numerous wrappings from a large inanimate object, which very much resembled a sleeping infant several months old. Helena's olive cheek glowed with a sudden flush like the rosy side of a ripe peach. She bent low over the object, which was now quite free from its protecting wraps, as she answered, "I suppose you will think me terribly silly; mamma said she was afraid the girls would make sport of me, if I brought it with me, but when I came away I found I just could not leave my dear dolly at home. Papa gave it to me three years ago Christmas, and I think it is the loveliest creature I ever saw in the shape of a doll. I have been so fond of her, and I have always had her in my room at night; and it broke my heart to think of leaving her behind me. So at last mamma said I might bring her. I shall keep her in the bottom drawer of the dresser, and no one but you need know she is here. I don't want the whole school laughing at me; but I know I shall be a great deal happier because she is with me. Did you feel badly when you had to give up your dolls?"

"I never played with a doll in all my life," Dolores answered, "I always knew they were only dolls."

"Yes, of course real babies are nicer, but they cry so, and one has to be so careful"

"Real babies!" echoed Dolores, in undisguised contempt, "I am sure I never want to play with those miserable little beings. I never know what to do with them."

"Don't you love babies? the sweet innocent little creatures," cried Helena, clasping her arms over an imaginary infant, and cuddling it to her breast with true mother-tenderness. "Oh, I think they are the loveliest, dearest little things in the world. How can you dislike them?"

"I don't really dislike them," Dolores replied; "I only pity them. Nobody ever asks them whether or not they wish to come into this world of trouble, nobody ever wants them, and everybody tires of their plaintive protest against life. Yes, indeed, I pity the poor things."

"Oh, but I am sure some babies are wanted," Helena interposed. "A little brother came to me three years ago, and we were all so glad and happy, as if an angel had been sent to us. And it was an angel," she added, in a lower tone, "for it was called back to heaven in a few months, and we were left so very, very lonely. But we were glad it came even for that brief time. It made us all better, I know. Have you any brothers or sisters, Dolores?"

"No," Dolores answered, "my mother died when I was six months old."

"Oh," said Helena, very softly, "then you are an orphan? I think that is the saddest thing in the world, to have no father and mother on earth."

"My father is living, but he has another wife, and I never see him," Dolores explained, "and I feel that I am an orphan. I live with my mother's brother, my Uncle Laurence, when I am at home. But I think we ought to retire early to-night, Miss Lena, you look very tired; this has been a hard day for you."

As they disrobed together, Helena's admiration for her companion's beauty broke forth again.

"You have the loveliest hair I ever saw," she said. "How I would love to see a picture of you with it flowing about your shoulders like that."

As malice creates malice, so generosity awakens generosity. Dolores, who was usually quite too indifferent to individuals to particularly notice, much less mention their pleasing traits, now smilingly replied to Helena's eulogy:

"And I would like a picture of your beautiful neck and shoulders; you have the form of a young goddess, my dear."

"Have I?" cried Helena with childish delight, "why, I am sure no one ever said so before, only Papa told me there was a classic slope to my shoulders, I always remembered that compliment, as I shall yours. I just worship beauty, and I am so grateful to heaven for the least little spark of prettiness it has given me, and I try to make the most of myself in every way. I think the Creator meant all women to be lovely; Eve was beautiful, I am sure; and it is only by disobeying the laws of health, and not thinking the right thoughts that her descendants have grown deformed and unattractive. That is what Mamma thinks, and I believe it is true too."

"Are you quite ready to retire," asked Dolores, as she saw Helena let down her brown hair over her snowy night-dress. "If so, I will put out the light."

"Oh dear, no," laughed Helena, "you have no idea how long a time I require at my toilet night and morning. You know I told you I tried to make the most of myself every way. Now nature did not give me much beauty to begin with, but Mamma says I can greatly improve on what was given me. My hair is not very fine or soft, so I give it a hundred strokes of the brush every night, and fifty every morning. Then I take ever so much pains with my teeth and nails, for they are very obvious features, you know, and my nails are inclined to be ugly, not naturally long and shapely like yours. And I am so fond of bathing, that Mamma says she ought to keep me in an aquarium with the gold fish."

"But you will find it very difficult to get time for so many elaborate ceremonies here at school," said Dolores.

"Well, then I shall fall behind in my classes, I fear," answered Helena as she stroked her hair till it glistened like the coat of a finely-groomed horse. "I look on my body as the temple of my soul, and I feel as if I was showing respect to God by taking every delicate and beautiful care of it that is possible. I do not care for fine clothes so much as some girls do, but I love to beautify and purify myself, the body that God made, and dedicate it anew to his service each day and night. What other girls spend in sweetmeats and candies, I use to buy delicate perfumes, and soaps, and dainty brushes and appliances for my toilet and bath. In fact, I suppose I am a born old maid. There now, you can put out the light, and hereafter I will take that task upon myself and not keep you waiting."

And then she dropped on her knees by the snowy couch in the moonlight, and offered up her simple silent prayer of petition and gratitude.

"A nice sweet girl," thought Dolores as she lay and watched the kneeling figure. "I think I shall quite enjoy her society."

And she did not dream that in the mercifully veiled future circumstances should transpire, which would cause her to feel for that same girlish figure kneeling at her bed-side, all the bitter hatred, all the passionate fury, all the jealous vengeance of which the human heart is capable when in the grasp of an immortal sorrow and a great despair.

CHAPTER III. A FATAL IMPRESS

Almost six months had flown, and the spring vacation was close at hand.

Helena's homesickness had given place to quiet content; and a keen pleasure in her new duties was fast taking possession of her, which Madame Scranton noticed with satisfaction, and reported to Mrs. Maxon.

"I dread vacation week," she said to her room-mate, one evening as they sat over their examination papers. "I was so lonely during the holidays while you were gone, I cried myself to sleep every night, and it will be just as hard this vacation. It seems a long time until next June, but I know my parents do not feel like affording the expense of my journey home before then."

"I wish you might go home with me," suggested Dolores, looking up suddenly from her books. "Can't you? it is only a short distance, and I would gladly take you myself. It is rather a gloomy house, you will find, with just uncle and his books, and servants, but it would be a change for you at least. I know how dreary it is here in vacation; I tried it once, when uncle was away from home. Will you go with me, Lena?"

"You are so kind to ask me, and I think it would be delightful," Helena answered, her face beaming at the thought. "I will write to Mamma about it to-night. I am sure she will give her consent, for I have told her so much about you, how good and kind you are, and how fond I am of you;" and Helena drew her companion's face down with both hands and kissed her. Dolores received the salutation with a smile, but did not return it.

"Do you know, Dolores," said Helena, "that little smile of yours means just the same to me now, as a kiss? At first, when I used to caress you, your lack of responses chilled me; yet I was so fond of you, and you are so lovely, I could not refrain from demonstrations of affection. I must have someone to pet; it is a necessity with me; and now that faint little smile you give me, seems just the same as a kiss would seem from any other girl."

"I am glad it does, it means the same," Dolores replied. "I am very undemonstrative by nature. You are positively the only person, Lena, by whom I could endure to be caressed. I do not remember that I ever voluntarily kissed any one in my life. I could never see any meaning or sense in it; but it seems all right coming from you. Only I am glad you do not demand a response from me."

"But surely you kiss your uncle sometimes?" Helena queried.

"No, never. His nature and mine are similar in that respect. You will think him cold, and severe, but he has had some bitter sorrows in his life, and it is no wonder if they have frozen his heart's blood. Yet he is very kind to me, and he has taught me much, and told me many things, which I might otherwise have had to learn as he did by cruel experience. But come, dear, we must finish our examination papers, and you must write that letter to your mother. I think I will enclose a note, begging her to grant me the favor of your company, and promising to take the best of care of you."

Both letters were accordingly written and an affirmative reply to the request was received by the delighted girls before the school term closed.

Helena packed her trunk with all a young girl's eager anticipation of a new experience. Madame Scranton and a small body-guard of teachers and pupils accompanied the young ladies to the depot, and saw them safely seated in the car which would, in a few hours, bring them to their destination.

They were met at the station by a colored serving man, whom Dolores addressed as Daniel, and who informed her that "Master Laurence was well nigh sick: did not seem to have no appetite and couldn't sleep."

"Why was I not written to? Why was I not sent for, if Uncle is ill?" cried Dolores, with so much distress in her face, that Helena, accustomed to the usual calm of her friend's demeanor, looked upon her with surprise.

Daniel's assurance that his master was not sick, "only ailin'," did not remove the cloud from Dolores' face until they reached the mansion, which seemed to Helena, filled with a "well-bred gloom," as she afterwards expressed it.

As a garment becomes impregnated with the odors of the body, so the atmosphere of a house becomes saturated with the essence or the spiritual nature of its inhabitants. In Helena Maxon's own home, humble and modest though it was, who ever crossed its threshold felt the rush of a vitalized current of love and good cheer, like a soft breeze about him.

And with her peculiarly sensitive nature she felt, like a finely organized human barometer, the cold and chilling atmosphere of this mansion: and her spiritual mercury ran down to the zeros.

A tall, grave man, with a clear-cut, beardless face and steel gray eyes, met them in the hall, "Welcome home, young ladies," he said, while the phantom of a smile played over his pale features, as a winter sunbeam falls on a marble statue. "I am glad to see you both. Dolores, child, you look pale; are you ill?"

He took her hand, as he had taken Helena's, and he offered no more affectionate greeting, nor did Dolores.

"No, I am well," she said, "only Daniel frightened me: he said you were very unwell. You should have sent for me, Uncle, at once."

"It was not necessary, child," replied her uncle, as he led them down the long hall and stood aside to let them pass up the broad stairway. "I have only been indisposed, as I always am in the Spring, you know. Why should I take you from your studies because my liver is refractory? But hasten, now, young ladies. You have only time to make your toilet before dinner is served."

"I heard two robins chirping in a bare tree this morning," Mr. Laurence said, as the young ladies took their places at the table a little later. "That and your youthful voices in the lonely old hall just now, convinced me of the near approach of Springtime. Happy birds, and happy girls, I said. I wonder what the brief summer of life holds for you?

"What is your dream of the future, Miss Maxon?"

Finding this perplexing question addressed to her so suddenly, by an utter stranger, whose demeanor gave her a peculiar sensation of awe, Helena blushed, and hesitated for a reply.

"I think I can answer for you," continued her host, without waiting for her to find voice.

"It is a dream of pleasant duties, of culture and travel, of realized ambitions and labors rewarded, but all merging in the supreme hope of the unwise young heart, love and marriage; am I not right?"

For a moment, Helena remained in abashed silence, the flush deepening upon her cheek. Then she lifted her soft dark eyes fearlessly to the old man's face, as she answered him:

"I have never thought very seriously about my future," she said. "I am young to make plans. But whatever else it holds for me, I think it would be more complete at last to be crowned with love and marriage, if the love were true love and the marriage a happy one."

Mr. Laurence shook his head as he murmured: "Ah! ah! poor child, poor foolish child! Better give up this thought at once. There is no true love between man and woman; there are no happy marriages; it is all a dream, a dream, and the awakening is cruel. Better put it all out of your mind now, child, before it is too late. Build your castle without the frail tower of love, else it will topple to the ground and carry the whole structure with it."

"But surely you would not have me think there is no such thing as true love in the world?" cried Helena, in wondering and pained surprise.

"There is no true and enduring love, no grand eternal passion between the sexes. There is a possibility, yet that even is rare, of a lasting platonic affection, of a kind, unselfish friendship. But it is a mockery and blasphemy for two human beings to stand at the altar and in the name of God bind themselves to be true to a sentiment which cannot last, which never lasts. One or both must change, both must suffer from the unholy bondage. Women are fickle, and men are base. I would rather see Dolores, my only human tie, laid in her grave, than led to the marriage altar. No, no, child; listen to an old man who has seen much of the world, and let no thought of marriage ever enter your life plans."

Mr. Laurence's face was very pale, and his voice trembled with the excitement which this subject always produced. Dolores saw that he was in a highly nervous state, and adroitly changed the conversation by requesting Helena to come into the music room and sing for them.

She possessed a voice of remarkable beauty and sweetness, a voice which already was beginning to develop into wonderful flexibility and power, under the vocal training she received at the Academy.

Like most of Orpheus' devotees, Helena was much more absorbed in the music than in the words of her songs; and so, quite unconsciously she illustrated the old man's theory of the ephemeral nature of love, in her selection of this song, which was set to a brilliant air and accompaniment.

A little leaf just in the forest's edge, All summer long, had listened to the wooing Of amorous birds that flew across the hedge, Singing their blithe sweet songs for her undoing. So many were the flattering things they told her, The parent tree seemed quite too small to hold her.

At last one lonesome day she saw them fly Across the fields behind the coquette summer, They passed her with a laughing light good-by, When from the north, there strode a strange new comer; Bold was his mien, as he gazed on her, crying, "How comes it, then, that thou art left here sighing!"

"Now by my faith thou art a lovely leaf. May I not kiss that cheek so fair and tender?" Her slighted heart welled full of bitter grief, The rudeness of his words did not offend her. She felt so sad, so desolate, so deserted, Oh, if her lonely fate might be averted.

"One little kiss," he sighed, "I ask no more" His face was cold, his lips too pale for passion. She smiled assent; and then bold Frost leaned lower, And clasped her close, and kissed in lover's fashion. Her smooth cheek flushed to sudden guilty splendor, Another kiss, and then complete surrender.

Just for a day she was a beauteous sight, The world looked on to pity and admire This modest little leaf, that in a night Had seemed to set the forest all on fire. And then this victim of a broken trust A withered thing, was trodden in the dust.

Mr. Laurence sat silent as if buried in deep thought, while she sang a few songs, and then, excusing himself on a plea of indisposition, retired to his room.

"It is useless for Uncle to tell me he is not ill," Dolores remarked, after he had left them alone, "for I notice a great change in him since I last saw him. He looks years older, and he is in a state of great nervousness. I am alarmed about him."

"He is a strange man, is he not?" mused Helena, "but I can not help thinking he would be happier and healthier if he did not live alone. If he had married when young, and was now surrounded by a nice family, how different all his ideas would be. Papa says a bachelor's blood turns to vinegar because he has no one to sweeten life for him."

"But Uncle Laurence is not a bachelor," Dolores said. "He married a very beautiful girl when he was quite young."

"Indeed! then he is a widower? And it was the loss of her, that made him so bitter! But I think it is lovely that he has been true to her memory. There is just romance enough about it to please me."

"No, no!" interrupted Dolores, hastily, "you do not understand. He married her and worshiped her, with a young man's first poetic passion;

they lived together two years, and then, and then, Lena, she ran off and left him, and he has never been the same man since."

"Ran off and left him!" echoed Helena in shocked amazement, "why, was she homesick, or was he unkind to her? And did her parents take her back?"

"No, she did not go home. She was, oh, Lena dear, you are too innocent to understand how wicked the world is. I know all about it, because Uncle has told me; he thinks it better for me to be forewarned since I may be left alone to defend myself. Lena, his wife was faithless, and his nearest friend false, and two homes were disgraced forever."

"Oh!" was Helena's only response. She was puzzled and pained to find the world not all like the sweet and holy atmosphere of her own home. But she felt sure that Mr. Laurence's life was a great exception to the rule, which must be peace, harmony and purity in the domestic relations.

As the two girls stood in the pale blue bower which was Dolores's apartment, disrobing for the night, Helena noticed a photograph album lying near at hand. "May I look at the pictures?" she asked, and as she turned the leaves, she uttered an exclamation of delight as her eyes fell on the photograph of a beautiful child, a boy seemingly four or five years old.

"Oh, Dolores, what a cherub! who is this?" she asked. "He is a perfect beauty, and he has your lovely mouth too, is he a relative?"

Dolores leaned over her shoulder and looked at the portrait.

"That? Oh, that is my father's little boy," she said indifferently. "The picture was sent me from California several years ago."

"But I thought you told me you had no brothers or sisters," said Helena, with a puzzled look.

Dolores ran her slender fingers through her silken hair, shaking it down about her like a golden halo.

"Well, I have none," she replied. "I am my mother's only child. He is my father's child, and one is not very much related to one's father any way, you know, and surely not at all to his children by another mother."

"Why, Dolores King!" cried Helena, now thoroughly shocked. "What strange things you are saying! Not related to one's father? Why, it is just as near and sacred a relation as that of a mother."

"Oh, no! child," interrupted Dolores. "Just think what a mother suffers for us, endures for us, goes through for us, from first to last. From the moment we begin to exist, until we can walk alone, we are a physical drain upon our mothers: while our fathers walk free and untrammeled, with only perhaps (and perhaps not even that) the thought of our maintenance to remind them that we have claims upon them. It is only a matter of association and personal pride, which endears most children to their fathers, while their mothers love them naturally. I have never lived with my father, since I was a small infant. I was placed in the care of a nurse, after my mother died, and then my father married again very soon, and my uncle took me home. I am sure my father has no affection for me, and I have none for him. I have seen him but a few times in my life, and I found him in no way attractive to me, and then I always remember how unhappy my mother's brief life was with him, and that makes me almost hate him. So, I am glad we do not meet oftener."

"Oh, Dolores," sighed Helena, looking at her beautiful companion with eyes of absolute compassion, "I think it is terrible for you to feel like this towards your own father. I cannot understand it."

"Well," confessed Dolores, pausing in the tasks of brushing her hair, and looking, in her dainty white robes, as Aphrodite clothed in mist might have looked had she risen from the sea with an ivory hair brush in her hand; "well, sometimes I cannot understand it either. But I once saw a girl with a queer mark on her brow, like the gash of a dagger; and I was told that it was caused by her father being struck down by a robber, right before her mother's eyes. And when I read my mother's diary, kept during her one year of married life, I think may be I was marked mentally, just that way. I suppose such a thing is possible; and I can no more help my feelings than the girl could help having the mark on her brow."

Dolores had struck a deeper truth than she imagined. But Helena's mind was not able to grasp it. She only felt that her friend was more and more of an enigma, and crept into bed with her brain in a state of chaotic confusion, bordering upon fear.

CHAPTER IV. A STARTLING VALEDICTORY

While the household slumbered a pale messenger entered silently and said to one of its members, "This night thy soul is required of thee! Come with me."

Mr. Laurence was found dead in his bed in the morning, a smile, warmer than his living features had worn for years, frozen upon his lips.

For those who have witnessed the ghastly spectacle of a modern funeral, no description of that barbarous rite is necessary. Who has not seen it all, the darkened room, stifling with its mingled odors of flowers and disinfectants; the sombre, hideous casket; the awful ceremony of screwing down the lid over the beloved face: the black army of pall-bearers: the long, slow, mournful journey to the desolate, disease-breeding cemetery; the damp, dark, yawning pit, the lowered coffin, the sickening thud of the earth as dust returns to dust. Oh! could the most savage race invest death with more terrors than this frightful custom of the civilized world? Then follows the long process of decay, the darkness, the gloom, the weight of the earth upon that dear breast, the grave-worm slowly eating his slimy way into the flesh which has thrilled under our warm kisses, God! are we not cruel to our dead?

Compare with this the beautiful ceremony of cremation. A snowy cloth envelopes the dead. A door swings open noiselessly, and the iron cradle, with its burden clothed as for the nuptial bed, rolls through the aperture and disappears in a glory of crimson light, as a dove sails into the summer sunset skies and is lost to view. There is no smoke, no flame, no odor of any kind. Nothing comes in contact with the precious form we have loved, but the purity of intense heat, and the splendor of great light. In a few hours, swiftly, noiselessly, with no repulsive or ghastly features in the process, the earthly part of our dear one is reduced to a small heap of snowy ashes. All hail the dawn of a newer and higher civilization, which shall substitute the cleanliness and simplicity of cremation for the complicated and dreadful horrors of burial!

By Mr. Laurence's will it was discovered that his entire property, amounting to a comfortable competence, belonged to Dolores, with the exception of the homestead: This was to pass into the hands of Dr. Monroe, his family physician and only intimate acquaintance. Friends offered the shelter of their homes to Dolores, and urged her to accept their sympathetic hospitality until her future plans were formed. But the sorrowing orphan refused to leave the thrice gloomy house. She clung to Helena, and said, between her sobs, "They tell me I must go away from here soon, forever: that it is no longer my home. Surely, I may remain a little while, a few weeks, and surely you will stay with me, Helena? I cannot leave it all so suddenly, it is too much to ask of me."

Finally it was decided that Dr. and Mrs. Monroe should take immediate charge of their new home, and that Helena should remain with her friend until her preparations were completed for a final departure.

Then together they would return to Madame Scranton's to remain until the June vacation, when Dolores would receive her diploma as a "finished" young lady.

One day Dolores asked Helena to assist her in selecting and packing the books she wished to take from her uncle's library. According to his will, she was to retain such portion of his collection as she most valued.

"All those on the second and lower shelves you may take down," she said. "They are my favorites, they have helped to form my mind and principles, and they seem like personal friends to me, and far more reliable than most people."

Helena read the titles of the books as she dusted them off and placed them in the packing boxes.

There were all the works of Chas. Fourier, Histories of all the Communistic Societies of ancient and modern times; all of George Sand's Works, Voltaire, Shelley, his life and works; Life of Mary Wollstonecraft, and her "Vindication of the Rights of Women;" Onderdonk's "Marriage prohibited by the Laws of God;" Balzac's "Petty Annoyances of Married Life;" "Disadvantages of the Married State," an antique book bearing the date of 1761; works by Mitchell and J. Johnson on the same subject; and many others by obscure authors. With the exception of a few, they were nearly all books of which Helena had never even heard. She glanced through the pages of Fourier, and sighed.

"Dear me!" she said, "how very much deeper your mind is than my own, Dolores. I could never in the world read such books as those; I could never become interested in them. I do not think I ever knew another person so wise as you are for your age."

"I take no credit to myself," Dolores answered; "it is all the result of my Uncle's training. 'As the twig is bent, the tree is inclined.' And yet I think my Mother's diary prepared me for this train of thought as nothing else could have done. Someday, Lena, I shall show you that diary; and then you will better comprehend me, and my ideas. But not yet; your mind is too child-like to grasp such sad truths. And still, I think they can scarcely be brought to our knowledge too soon."

Helena's curiosity was aroused, and her first impulse was to ask Dolores for the diary, or at least to urge her to reveal something of the nature of its contents. But a second thought caused her to respond in an entirely different way.

"I should wish to have my Mother read the diary first," she said, "if it contains any information on matters of which I am now ignorant. I am sure she would be the best judge, whether or not I need such instruction. She has always told me to come first to her for explanation of anything which surprised or puzzled me. I am sure she would not approve if I disobeyed her in this instance."

"You are quite right, Lena," her friend answered, with a sense of having been quietly rebuked. "I know I have talked too freely with you on this matter; I have excited your curiosity, and to no good result. But somehow, I talk to you more unreservedly than I ever conversed with anyone else. I don't know why; I have always prided myself on my reticence, yet your sweet sympathy seems to destroy my caution. I respect your delicate idea of what is due your mother, and I will not thrust my heart's convictions upon you again, dear."

Still, it was owing to Helena's own sense of honor, that Dolores had not startled and shocked her young and perfectly innocent mind, by unfolding unlovely facts, and rude truths, for which she was totally unprepared. Yet, Madame Scranton had assured Mrs. Maxon, that Miss King was an admirable companion for her young daughter. So poorly does the most careful preceptor, as a rule, understand the complex natures in her care, and so little does the most prudent parent realize the dangers to which she exposes her daughter in these boarding-school intimacies.

It seemed to Helena, that she was years older, and sadder, when, at the expiration of three weeks, she accompanied Dolores back to Madame Scranton's Academy.

The sudden death of Mr. Laurence, upon the very night of her arrival, the gloom of the succeeding days, the heart-breaking sorrow of Dolores, as she bade a last adieu to the old house, and went forth homeless, though an heiress, all served to sadden and depress Helena's usually buoyant spirits.

"I am glad I went home with Dolores," she wrote to her mother, "both because the poor girl needed me in her time of trouble, and because it has made me more than ever grateful to heaven for the blessings of my dear parents, and my happy home. Poor Dolores! she has a fortune, and great personal beauty, and a wonderfully deep mind; you would be surprised, Mamma, to see the books that girl has read. But she has no home, no mother, and my heart aches for her. For some strange reason, she seems to feel a repugnance, that is almost hatred, towards her father, who is living, you know. She says, when I read her mother's diary, that I will understand her better. She puzzles me very much, she says such strange things. But I am very fond of her, Mamma, and I want you to invite her to come home with me, after she graduates. Just think! she has no place on earth she can call home. Is it not a terribly sad situation for a girl like her?" So it was decided that Dolores should accompany her friend to Elm Hill, at the close of the term.

Perhaps Mrs. Maxon might have hesitated, in writing the sweet motherly letter of invitation which she sent to Dolores, if she had seen the manuscript upon which that young lady was hard at work: the manuscript of the address she was to deliver, "Commencement Day."

Mrs. Maxon was present when that day arrived. Fair girls in snowy costumes fluttered upon the stage of the assembly hall, like a shower of apple-blossoms; delivered themselves of pretty platitudes, and time-worn sentiments, in sweet treble voices: were listened to, and applauded, by proud parents and admiring friends, and made their graceful exit, no longer school-girls, but young ladies fully equipped for "Society."

All but one. She came, clothed in deepest mourning, with only a cluster of purple pansies to relieve the dead blackness of her garments, out of which rose like a star from midnight clouds her beautiful, pallid face, with its crown of golden hair.

Perfect silence reigned in the Assembly Hall, when Dolores began speaking. Her voice was clear as the tones of a silver bell, her pronunciation distinct and deliberate. Her theme was, "Woman, her Duties and her Dangers." In terse and finely chosen sentences, she denounced marriage as a bondage and slavery, of the most degrading type, opposed to the highest interest of Society as a whole, and of women in particular. She quoted liberally from various authors, to substantiate her assertions, and closed with an eloquent appeal to all her classmates, to avoid this dangerous pitfall; to go forth into world self-reliant and strong in their determination to make places and homes for themselves, untrammeled by indissoluble and uncongenial companionships. Although making her assertions with most startling positiveness, her choice language conveyed no offensive phrases. But the address, on the whole, was so socialistic, and its ideas so unfeminine and extreme, that it feel, if not like a bomb-shell, at least like a small torpedo, in that assemblage of conventional maidens and matrons. And Dolores beautiful and brilliant, and (if too reserved to be a favorite), at least the most admired and envied of her class, retired from the platform amidst a profound silence.

Madame Scranton felt deeply mortified at the conduct of her model pupil. She had known the title of Dolores's address, but having such unlimited faith in that young lady's discretion, and ability, she had not deemed it necessary to inspect the manuscript. Other pupils needed her attention, and she felt confident that Miss King would deliver a masterly effort, one which would reflect credit upon herself and the Academy. Dolores invariably did well. Madame was aware, that she had contracted some severe prejudices against marriage; that she was, in fact, almost a man-hater. But these ideas would no doubt wear away, in contact with the world. She had not the slightest knowledge of their strong, tenacious hold upon Dolores's mind, until she sat in shocked surprise, and listened to her startling oration.

So soon as her duties would permit, Madame hastened to make her apologies to Mrs. Maxon.

"I fear you will distrust my judgment," she said, "in placing your daughter in close companionship with that young lady. But really, the strange outburst from Miss King is wholly unaccountable to me. I cannot understand where she contracted such ideas."

"I think I can," Mrs. Maxon answered, quietly, remembering Helena's references to her friend in her letters. "I am about to take the young lady home with me, and I hope I can rid her of some of her morbid ideas. It is well for young ladies to make marriage a secondary, not the first consideration of life; but it is very unfortunate to view the matter through Miss King's diseased eyes. There must be some cause for her peculiar state of mind. I shall try and fathom it."

CHAPTER V. A YOUNG CYNIC.

Mrs. Maxon sat on the pleasant veranda of her home, at Elm Hill, with a snowy piece of needlework in her hands.

Mr. Maxon lounged back in a rustic chair, smoking a fragrant cigar.

Dolores swung lazily in a hammock nearby, a beautiful picture of indolent repose.

From within, floated a rarely musical voice in snatches of song:

The day is drawing near, my dear, When you and I must sever; Yet whether near or far we are, Our hearts will love forever, Our hearts will love forever.

O sweet, I will be true, and you Must never fail or falter; I hold a love like mine divine, And yours, it must not alter, O, swear it will not alter.

She sang the simple words to a light flowing air, with a rippling accompaniment. Then, suddenly striking rich chords of harmony, she broke into a song that might have served well as a passionate response to the other ditty:

I will be true. Mad stars forsake their courses, And, led by reckless meteors, turn away From paths appointed by Eternal Forces. But my fixed heart shall never go astray. Like those calm worlds, whose sun-directed motion Is undisturbed by strife of wind or sea, So shall my swerveless, and serene devotion Sweep on forever, loyal unto thee.

I will be true. Light barks may be belated, Or turned aside by every breeze at play; While sturdy ships, well manned, and richly freighted, With broad sails flying, anchor safe in bay. Like some firm rock, that, steadfast and unshaken, Stands all unmoved, while ebbing billows flee, So would my heart stand, faithful if forsaken. I will be true, though thou art false to me.

"How wonderfully Lena's voice has improved during the last year;" Mrs. Maxon said, with motherly pride, as the song ceased. "And she sings, too, with great feeling; do you not think so, Miss King? She seemed to throw so much intensity into those words just now, as if they came from her very heart."

"She has a remarkably magnetic voice; and one that stirs the best impulses of her listeners," Dolores answered. "I am peculiarly susceptible to different kinds of music. A violin appeals to the artistic and spiritual part of me. A pipe-organ stirs the dramatic and sorrowful side of my nature. A violin lifts up my thoughts towards the Celestial City that awaits me. An organ makes me wonder why this tragic life was ever thrust upon my unwilling soul. Helena's voice affects me in still another way. Whenever I hear her sing, I feel a curious uprising of all my mental powers, of all my moral forces. It seems to me there is nothing I can not do, and be. It is only one voice in a thousand which can affect me in this manner."

"I understand what you mean," Mrs. Maxon replied. "I have heard nearly all our public singers, and among them all Emma Abbott's voice possessed for me more of this peculiar quality, which you rightly term magnetic, than any of her no doubt greater rivals. I think it is derived from the electric temperament of the singer; and it is almost always associated with an unselfish nature. But what ever its cause, it is a great gift."

"Yes, and one which no amount of training or culture can supply if it is denied by nature. But do you know, I feel provoked with Lena, when she wastes the music of her lovely voice on such sentiments as those songs contained?"

"There you go prancing off on your hobby again," laughed Helena, who emerged from the house just in time to hear Dolores's closing sentence. "Can't you let me sometimes indulge in a little sentiment in my music, dear?"

"And what nobler themes for song can you find, Dolores?" Mrs. Maxon asked gently, "than love, faith, and loyalty. They are the foundations of the world and society."

"But it seems so foolishly absurd for two people to swear to love each other forever!" Dolores continued, with a touch of scorn in her voice. "No doubt they often believe it possible, but one or the other is sure to falter; and then a broken oath renders the human weakness of change a sin. I do not believe that two people should pledge themselves to love forever. We cannot compel a sentiment or an emotion to remain with us, after it chooses to depart. We can, of course, compel ourselves to live up to its requirements, through principle, though this would be dreary work, I fancy. Yet it is the situation of half the married couples in the world. Love flies, and takes with him all the real pleasures they found in each other's society. Yet they plod along, in a compulsory sort of fashion, doing their duty, ugh; it is horrible to think of. Society is all wrong."

Mrs. Maxon dropped her work and looked at Dolores with a compassionate glance.

"You must admit that there are many exceptions to your rule, Dolores," she said. "Surely your month in our home ought to convince you that love has abided here through many years."

"Yes, I am very sure of that," Dolores admitted. "But your life is an exceptional one in this respect. You know the old mythological tale of the creation of souls? An angel stands beside a liquid sea, dipping in a long pole. Upon its point he brings up a perfect globule: it contains two souls, affinities. He gently shakes the pole, and one half rolls away: he shakes it again, and away rolls the other in an opposite direction. Day and night, for weeks, months, years, centuries, he plies his task, while the separated globules increase, and multiply, and go rolling about the world seeking their affinities. So innumerable in numbers, and so similar in appearance, it is no wonder if mistakes occur in the selections they make. The only wonder is, that one in a million actually finds its own half. You, madame, are an illustration, that such a miracle is possible, and I congratulate you. But the dreary outlook remains for the majority."

Mr. Maxon removed his cigar and laughed heartily at the young lady's bright response.

"You are incorrigible," he said. "Mrs. Maxon, it is useless to endeavor to worst Miss King in argument. Just wait till Prince Charming appears, however, and see how easily he will convince her that their souls were originally one perfect globule. And she will promise to love, honor, and obey, forever, without a murmur."

"Never!" cried Dolores, springing to her feet. "I will never become the wife of any man, I have solemnly sworn it. I would as soon be sold into slavery. I can imagine no fate more humiliating to a proud woman, than that of a neglected or unloved wife," and she abruptly entered the house.

There came a time when she realized the possibility of a fate more humiliating.

That night, as Mrs. Maxon sat in her room alone, overlooking some linen, Dolores tapped gently at her door.

She came forward in answer to Mrs. Maxon's bidding, her lovely hair flowing over her white garments, her face pale with suppressed emotion.

"Mrs. Maxon, I have brought you my mother's diary to read," she said. "I think it will help you to better understand my ideas on the subject of marriage. No eyes save my uncle's and my own have ever perused its pages. But I want you to see it, that you may understand me more fully." And, placing the little journal in Mrs. Maxon's hand, she glided away.

The following morning Dolores received a letter which brought the most unexpected changes in her life. This was the letter:

"N. Y. CITY, July 30, 18--.

"MISS DOLORES KING:

"It is quite possible you may have heard your uncle, Mr. Laurence, speak of Sarah Winters. I was at one time an intimate friend of your mother's before her marriage. After her death I called twice to see you, her baby orphan. Then I married and lost track of you during several years. Recently the news of your uncle's death and your second bereavement reached me accidentally. I made inquiries and learned that you had graduated from Madame Scranton's Academy, and, though possessed of a competence, that you were entirely without a home. Now I will tell you my object in addressing you. Several years ago I was left a widow, and without means. During my youth and early married life, I had lived much abroad. I was familiar with the Old World, and understood all the ins and outs, so to speak, of travel. And the idea suggested itself to me that I might bring my knowledge to a practical use. Consequently I became a professional chaperone for parties of ladies who desired to go abroad and see the greatest amount possible of the Old World, with the least expense. For a stated sum, I agree to conduct parties all through the most desirable portions of Europe, pay all the bills incident to travel, and return them safely to their native land. In ten days I sail with my fifth expedition, which consists of twenty ladies, for all of whom I vouch as to character and respectability. Would you not like to join us? I am anxious to renew my acquaintance with you, the orphaned child of my old friend and companion. For information concerning me, I refer you to Smith & Millet, Bankers; the Rev. Dr. Bradly, Rector of St. Paul's," &c., &c.

Then followed a long list of references, together with the terms for the expedition. The letter was signed Mrs. Sarah Butler.

Dolores passed the letter to Mr. and Mrs. Maxon for their perusal and opinion. "I remember hearing my uncle speak of Mrs. Butler," she said. "Her husband was a miserable drunkard, and wasted all her property in a dissipated career. I should love dearly to go abroad; it has been the dream of my life."

Accordingly, Mr. Maxon dispatched one or two letters of inquiry concerning Mrs. Butler, and received replies corroborating all her statements. And Dolores decided to accept this opportunity for travel under such excellent guardianship.

Since the death of her uncle, the future had seemed to her a shoreless sea, a waste of water with no green island in view. She had not found it possible to make any plans, but had accepted each day as it came, not daring to look beyond. Now she was thankful that another had planned for her. She wrote her acceptance to Mrs. Butler, and in a few days went out from the sweet rest and seclusion of this ideal home, forever.

She wept violently when parting from Helena, and clasped her again and again to the heart that would one day hate her with all the fury of a desperate soul at bay.

CHAPTER VI. A MOTHER'S VIEW OF "WOMAN'S RIGHTS"

Mrs. Maxon read the diary and returned it to Dolores the night previous to her departure. But in the hurry and excitement incident to the occasion, she found no suitable opportunity for a long motherly talk with the young lady, as she had hoped. She merely said, as she returned the book:

"I am glad you permitted me to read this, Dolores. It has enabled me to better understand your strange repugnance for marriage. Your mother was an unwilling parent, and your nature is impregnated with the rebellious feelings which filled her heart and brain. I hope you will outgrow them, however, and anchor yourself in a happy home. I could wish for you no greater joy than a married life as congenial and pleasant as my own."

After Dolores's departure, Helena referred to the subject of the diary.

"Dolores told me that you read it, Mamma, and I am really curious to know the contents of that mysterious book. She used to refer to it so often, and one time she would have shown it to me, because she said it contained truths which I ought to know; but I would not read it without your permission. Was Dolores's mother a greatly wronged woman, Mamma? and was her husband so very unkind to her? Dolores seemed to almost loathe his memory, and I fancied he must have been a very cruel man."

Mrs. Maxon took Helena's hand and drew her down on a low ottoman at her side. They were quite alone.

"No, my child," she said, gravely; "Mr. King was not a cruel man, and Mrs. King was not a greatly wronged woman. But their marriage was not a true and holy one, according to my idea of that sacred relation. In the early pages of the diary, written just before and just after the marriage, the young bride speaks constantly of her pride in having made a brilliant alliance. It seems she bettered her condition in a worldly sense, by her marriage, and it was this ambition, rather than a great love, which led to the union. During the first few months, the diary abounds with references to receptions, dinners, balls, where she had been admired and courted. Then begins a series of wild, despairing complaints against Providence and her husband and the world. Bitter, unreasoning denunciations of the marriage tie, and mournful regrets, as weak as useless, for her lost freedom. All this was occasioned by the knowledge that she was to become a mother. Her emotions seemed to culminate in violent anger toward her husband, and resentful wrath at a social system which she said was more brutal than the laws which govern brutes; since they are never compelled to bring undesired offspring into the world, with every instinct crying out against it. Almost insane with the intensity of these emotions, it is no wonder her daughter's mind was impressed with them. Now, my sweet child," continued Mrs. Maxon, drawing Helena closer to her side, "all this is very strange to you, I know, but it is a subject of vast importance to all our sex, to all the world; and I think you are at an age when you ought to understand it fully."

"That is what Dolores said, Mamma," interrupted Helena. "She said I ought to know these things, and she wanted me to read the diary."

"Yes, but I am glad you did not read it," her mother replied. "It would be like looking for a reflection of your own sweet face in a broken mirror. The diary presented important facts for your consideration, to be sure, but it presented them in a diseased and unnatural form. The subject of marriage and maternity, as treated in the diary, would have alarmed and shocked you, while in reality they are as sacred and beautiful as religion. It is of the utmost importance that our girls and women should think upon these subjects, and think of them as natural and holy events, before taking upon themselves the duties of wives and mothers. But it would have been a matter of lasting regret to me if you had gained your first ideas of these momentous questions from the diary. It is by her own mother a girl should be taught to understand these things in all their beauty and solemnity.

"In the case of Mrs. King, her first great error lay in the wrong motive which led to her marriage. It was ambition, not love or respect; and motherhood she regarded as a misfortune. She was evidently a woman of strong feeling, and therefore more capable of influencing the mind of her offspring. The child came into the world with the same intense hatred of the father, and rebellion against marriage, which had filled her mother's heart all these months."

"How very strange!" mused Helena, bewildered.

"Yes, strange, beautiful and terrible in the responsibility it places upon our sex, Helena. We make or mar the character of our offspring, often, by the thoughts we entertain during the prenatal period of their existence. You know I am an advocate for the widest education of woman; for her having all the doors of the professions, and arts, and trades, flung open to her, if she chooses to fit herself to enter them. Yet I am surprised and pained, often, as I see so many of the most interested and zealous workers in this cause, ignoring or misusing the grand and wonderful right and duty, ordained by heaven for woman, the right of moulding the mind, temper, and character of her children. You know, dear, do you not, the world-wide reputation which ancient Greece had in its glory for the beauty of its people?"

"Oh, yes. I learned all about that at school. The Greeks were the handsomest people, the most perfect, physically, I suppose, of any race which ever existed."

"Yes, that is true, Helena. And now let me tell you the cause of this. In Greece, a woman who was to become a mother was guarded from every annoyance, or pain, or peril; she was regarded by her husband, and by all men, as a divine being, chosen by God as a holy messenger from His very courts. She was surrounded by beautiful paintings, music, literature, and an atmosphere of love and homage. It is no wonder that the Greeks became the most beautiful people in the world. But as time passed, all this changed. Men failed to hold women in such reverence, and then Greece fell; and its glory, and the beauty of its people, became only a thing of the past. There is an old mythological tale that the soul of a man who maltreats a woman at this time goes into an owl's body when he dies, and remains there through three generations. But in our own country, I think women maltreat themselves more frequently. Every wrong impulse, every unkind thought or act that enters into a woman's heart, during this sacred period, should be guarded against and dispelled, with caution and with prayer. To listen to fine music, to look upon lovely objects, to enjoy agreeable surroundings, these things are not always within reach of a woman. But efforts at self-command, and an unselfish forethought for the future of the child, and prayer, the humblest can employ these means to the desired end. Prayer is the key to heaven. It admits us to the sacrament of angels. In God's vast Government he has constantly a deputy of angels who guard each human being. If we appeal to them, they redouble their efforts to help and strengthen us. If we neglect and ignore them, they finally grow disheartened and turn to more willing souls. It is my belief that there are no heights of moral grandeur we cannot attain, if we are vigilant in prayer. I want you to remember that many of our criminals, are the results of a mother's attempt to destroy her helpless child. The murderous impulse was imparted to the defenseless little creature, a seed that blossomed into rank crime. Many an unruly and defiant son, who breaks his mother's heart, by his disobedience and rebellion, could lay the cause at his mother's door.

"Never was a child more eagerly longed for than your own sweet self, Helena. My heart overflowed with happiness, all during those months of expectancy. As a consequence, your own nature is full of joy and sunshine, and you have been a comfort and a blessing to me always. Yet I was ignorant of any great responsibility at that time. Not till later in life did I obtain the knowledge, which is of far more value to our young women graduates, than all the horrors of vivisection with which so many of them are familiar.

"And now, good night, my daughter. Remember that these subjects should never be discussed lightly or irreverently; they are holy, and sacred, and beautiful; they are part of religion, for they pertain to the divine mysteries of our existence."

CHAPTER VII. THE LOVELY CYNIC MEETS HER FATE

Percy Durand looked out of the window of his compartment, as the train paused at Montivilliers, and lazily watched the people on the platform.

"There is nothing new under the sun," he yawned. "The world is monotonously alike, go where you will. There are always the same people hurrying to catch the train, and waiting until they can blockade the car steps before they bid a lingering farewell to friends. Then there are the same irritated and baggage-encumbered travelers waiting behind them, and cursing inwardly, and upon my soul, what a very pretty girl!"

This irrelevant finale to the idle reverie of the blasé Young American, was caused by the glimpse of a perfect profile, a coil of yellow hair and a gracefully-poised head under a jaunty hat, passing by the window. Percy Durand believed that he had exhausted nearly all his capabilities of enjoyment in this stale world. But his artistic appreciation of the beautiful still remained to him. The study of a handsome face, whether on man, woman, or child, was one of his greatest sources of pleasure.

Craning his neck to obtain another glimpse of the lovely vision, he was suddenly made aware that the door of his compartment had been thrown open, and that two ladies had entered.

One, the very object of his thoughts; the other, a fine-looking middle-aged lady, whose dignified expression suddenly gave place to a smile of recognition, as her eyes fell upon Percy.

"Why, surely this is Mr. Durand, Nora Tracy's Cousin 'Pierre,' is it not?" she said, holding out her hand. "Ah, I see you have forgotten me."

"No, indeed, Mrs. Butler, I have not!" cried Percy, giving the extended hand a thoroughly American "shake", not the polite touch of kid-covered finger-tips, but the cordial clasp that means so much to Americans meeting in a foreign land. "How could I forget the friend and chaperone of my dear cousin. Only yesterday, in a letter I received, she spoke of you, and said she hoped it might be my good fortune to run across you. It is a pleasure I hardly expected however."

Mrs. Butler, after acknowledging the speech with a few polite words, turned toward her companion.

"Let me introduce you to my protege," she said. "Mr. Durand: Miss King." And Percy looked into eyes as blue, and cold, as the waters of some quiet lake sleeping under a winter moon, and saw a face as faultlessly beautiful as the features of a marble goddess.

There was nothing romantic or unusual, in this very commonplace meeting between two people whose destinies were to be so tragically interwoven. Neither was powerfully impressed by, or drawn toward the other. There was no warning in either heart of the fate to come.

Dolores King, now in the perfection of her womanhood, matured by the experiences of travel, contact with the world, wide reading, and all the many advantages financial independence gives, regarded Mr. Percy Durand as a very good-looking typical American, in his late twenties. A little too thin and blond, perhaps, to suit her ideal of masculine beauty, but a man of fine address, and possessed of a wonderfully musical voice.

She felt a trifle more interest in him than she usually felt in the chance acquaintances Mrs. Butler was forever running across, from the fact that Nora Tracy, now Mrs. Phillips, who had been a great favorite and pet with Mrs. Butler, was his cousin.

Percy Durand admired the exquisite beauty of Miss King's face, the graceful dignity of her bearing, and quietly analyzed her after his usual custom, while he chatted with Mrs. Butler.

"A cold and reserved nature," he thought, "devoid of woman's usual vanity, proud to the verge of haughtiness, not susceptible to ordinary flattery; and she has never loved. When she does, God pity the man!"

Percy Durand was in the habit of regarding women, as students of the floral world regard flowers, and he botanized them in like manner. Many years ago, he had idealized the sex; but one woman's perfidy, together with the vanity and selfishness of many others, had served to disillusion him. Too finely fibered to ever become a bitter cynic, he was simply an amused skeptic on the subject of woman's superiority or moral worth. He had sought the world over for the ideal woman, that mythical personage of his early dreams. But he had found so much envy, jealousy, and selfishness marring the sex in general, he had discovered such unsightly blemishes on some of the most seemingly spotless natures, that he abandoned the search as hopeless.

"Not a marrying man," his friends said, when speaking of him. Handsome, eligible, and the junior member of a wealthy New York importing house, he was a desirable conquest for anxious damsels. But Percy Durand seemed either too heartless, or too selfish, to assume the rôle of Benedict.

"My cousin, Mrs. Phillips, will be anxious to know particulars concerning you, Mrs. Butler," he said, as they chatted together. "Are you chaperoning your usual bevy of young ladies this year?"

"Miss King has been my only charge for nearly four years," Mrs. Butler answered, smiling. "Five years ago, she joined a party of twenty young ladies under my charge. After a few months, she decided to remain abroad, and easily persuaded me to assume the position of companion and chaperone. We have led a delightful, bohemian sort of existence together. A year in Paris; winters in Rome, Genoa, Florence; summers in Northern Europe, in fact, journeying or lingering wherever my young friend's impulses led her. Just now we are en route for the Paris Exposition."

"And I also," said Percy, "with half the world. I hope you have engaged rooms. I fancy there will be a great rush, and much discomfort."

"Miss King had her usual apartments reserved for her. She left them all furnished when we went to Genoa. I hope if Nora, Mrs. Phillips I should say, comes abroad, she will come directly to us. We could make her very comfortable, could we not, Dolores?"

"Certainly," answered Dolores. "And I should be pleased to meet her. Mrs. Butler makes me almost jealous by her frequent references to your cousin, Mr. Durand."

"You are very kind; but Mrs. Phillips is not coming abroad this year. She is kept at home by her two children. She is the happiest wife and mother I ever saw. To a man of my skeptical ideas on the subject of marriage, the occasional sight of true domestic happiness, is all that saves me from absolute cynicism. Whenever I am tempted to doubt the existence of that congenial mating of two souls, of which we read so much, and see so little, I think of my cousin, and realize that it does exist, at least in one instance."

Just at this juncture, Miss King, who had begun to be absorbed in a book, leaving the two friends to chat, lifted her eyes with a slight amused smile in their depths.

"Pardon me," she said, "but how long has your cousin been married?"

"Four years." Percy answered.

"Ah! I fancied so. You see, she has hardly yet passed beyond the experimental period," laughed Dolores. "You know the serpent did not enter Paradise until sometime after it was created. But he always comes in one shape or another, and the Eden is always destroyed. It never lasts."

"Now you have touched upon Miss King's hobby, you see," Mrs. Butler said, in response to Percy's surprised look. "She is the most absolute cynic on the subject of love and marriage which the world contains, Mr. Durand. However, I live in hopes of her reformation. You know when unbelievers are converted, they make most devout worshipers."

"I shall never be converted from my settled convictions on this subject," Miss King replied, good naturedly. "There are people who are only fitted for a life of perfect freedom. I am one of them."

"And I, Miss King, am another!" added Percy. "A more confirmed bachelor never lived. Marriage seems to me a pitiful bondage, always for one, often for both. And a happy union is merely a fortunate accident. Whenever I hear the ringing of marriage bells, I think with Byron, that

'Each stroke peals for a hope the less, the funeral note Of love deep buried without resurrection In the grave of possession.'"

A smile that warmed her features like a burst of sunlight illumined Miss King's lovely face.

"I am sure we should agree famously on this subject, at least, Mr. Durand," she said. "It is seldom I meet a gentleman whose ideas accord so perfectly with my own."

"You are two foolish children," interposed Mrs. Butler, "and your ideas are quite too extreme. Marriage is not the wretched bondage you describe it. Someone has said very truthfully, 'If nothing is perfect in this world, marriage is perhaps the best thing amid much evil. If a fickle husband goes, he returns: but the lover, once gone he never returns.' I am sure, Mr. Durand, that you would make some woman an excellent husband."

Percy shook his head. "That is because you do not know me," he replied. "Whatever my nature was originally, my experiences in the world have left me incapable of unselfish devotion, or absorbing love."

"Oh, oh!" cried Mrs. Butler, "I will not hear you so malign yourself. Any man who was so kind as you were to your cousin, must have a heart."

"Perhaps I had, once upon a time. But there is such a thing as frittering away one's best emotions. Certainly, now, I cannot imagine a woman so good, so beautiful, or so endowed with graces, that I should wish to make her my wife. If I did, I know her goodness would be a reproach to me, her beauty would pall upon me, and her constancy would irritate me. And yet, the absence of any of these qualities would displease me. So you see I am better off single. I think my cousin considers me a good sort of relative! I am sure I am faithful in my friendships: but the requisites of a desirable husband, I do not possess. Besides, begging the pardon of both my lady listeners, I must say, while I have so little faith in myself, I have even less in womankind. I do not care to risk my future in the hands of an unreliable woman."

"A man of your experience and judgment would not be apt to make that error," Mrs. Butler replied. "And women are proverbially faithful by nature, you know, even clinging to the men who maltreat them."

"Judgment and experience are not of the slightest use in selecting a wife or husband," responded Percy. "First, because it is only in the daily intimacies of constant companionship that we can learn another's peculiarities; and secondly, in the case of the woman, at least, the maiden and wife are two distinct beings. I have seen the most amiable and charming girl develope into a veritable Xantippe of a wife. Then, as for the proverbial faithfulness of woman, it is the poet's idea of the sex, I know, but it is not verified in reality. Women are quite as faulty as men, and even more easily assailed by temptation. But they are more discreet, and make a greater show of good qualities than we do. Men boast of their infidelities, women conceal them."

"Rouen!" shouted the guard, flinging open the door of the compartment.

"Impossible!" cried Percy, springing up"and I am obliged to stop here! This is altogether too bad. But I hope you will kindly send your address to me at the Grand Hotel, where I shall register next week. I shall be glad to be of any service to you I can, during my few weeks in Paris."

And with that inimitable grace of the polished New Yorker, Percy bowed himself from the presence of the ladies.

And the first chapter was written in a romance which was to end in a tragedy.

CHAPTER VIII. SWEET DANGER

"My Dear," said Mrs. Butler, one morning at the breakfast table, ten days later, as she looked up from her letters to the vision of blonde loveliness opposite, "here is a note from Mr. Durand, the American gentleman we met, you remember. He is in Paris, and wishes to call."

"That is pleasant news," Dolores answered, smiling, "and I hope you will forward our united permission and compliments by return mail."

"Really, Dolores, you quite astonish me!" ejaculated Mrs. Butler. "When were you ever known to be so amiably disposed toward any gentleman before? What spell has Mr. Durand exercised over you, I wonder?"

"The spell of sincerity and good sense!" responded Dolores, as she sipped her coffee. "Two virtues so rare in mankind that it is no wonder if they left an indelible impression upon me. Mr. Durand is, almost without exception, the only gentleman I have met since my uncle died who did not feel it his duty to express, in words or manner, a disbelief in the sincerity of my views concerning marriage. You very well know, Mrs. Butler, how discouraging have been my attempts at friendship with the opposite sex, owing to this fact."

"Owing to your own charms, rather," Mrs. Butler corrected, "and to your hatred for the sex. Men are not easily satisfied with the cold indifference which you term friendship of a woman as fair as yourself."

"But I am not cold or indifferent to those who treat my opinions with respect," Dolores insisted. "And I am not a man-hater. I would like the companionship of men right well. I enjoy their society more than I enjoy the society of most women. They have broader views; they get outside of themselves far more than women do; they dwell less in their own emotions; and are, consequently, more interesting. But the selfishness, conceit and sensuality of men render them impossible friends for unprotected women."

"You must not include all men in that sweeping sarcasm, Dolores. There are exceptions."

"Possibly. I hope Mr. Durand is one. I speak of men as I have found them. You remember Clarence Walker, and how positive I was that I had found a loyal friend in him? And you know the result."

"Yes; he became madly in love with you. I do not see how either of those three condemnatory terms apply to him, however."

"But I do. Since he knew from the outset my firm resolve to never marry, he ought not to have allowed himself to think of me as a possible wife. But in his masculine conceit he really believed he could overcome the principles of a lifetime. Each man considers himself the Prince Charming, who holds the key to the enchanted palace of a woman's heart. Positively, the vanity of the sterner sex is colossal in its magnitude. Then, you know, there was Count D'Estey, with his really charming sister and picturesque mother. You remember my experience with him?"

"Certainly. He imagined you to be much wealthier than you are, my dear; and your fortune and your beauty were great temptations. It is no wonder he made an effort to win you. Foreign counts are born to be supported by American heiresses."

"And he ruined three delightful friendships by the futile effort. Yet that was the selfishness of the man's nature. Last of all, you know the result of my acquaintance with General Veddars?"

"Pardon me; but I do not. I only know that you returned from their country seat unexpectedly, joined me in London, and never referred to the subject of your acquaintance with the family again. I confess that I have often wondered what occurred to break up the intimacy which seemed so pleasant at one time."

"Well, then, I will tell you what happened," answered Dolores, with fine scorn in her face and voice. "Because I was outspoken and frank upon the subject of marriage, because I repeatedly declared that I should never be the wife of any man, General Veddars, it seems, imagined I was utterly lacking in mental and moral balance. At all events, he forgot himself, forgot that he was old enough to be my father, and that his wife was my devoted friend; and he embarrassed me with his attentions. Is it any wonder that I left his house, angry, shocked, and with a greater contempt for men and husbands than ever?"

Mrs. Butler shook her head. "There is no object in life more disgusting," she said, "than a man who carries the fires of an unlicensed youth into old age. I confess you have good cause to feel disappointed in your masculine friends. Let us hope that Mr. Durand will prove a success. One thing is certain, he comes of an excellent family; and he bears the best of reputations among men, and while he is not a ladies' man, he is very popular with our sex."

Dolores laughed lightly.

"The fact that his family is excellent, does not necessarily speak well for him," she said. "Many a low rascal on earth boasts of his noble ancestors under ground. And that he bears the best of reputations among men, is no proof that he may not be the worst companion possible for a woman. I am relieved to hear you say that he is not a ladies' man. That term always suggests to me a frivolous nature, something even more intolerable in a man than a woman. But really, ma chère, we are devoting more time to the discussion of this stranger, than is profitable. If we are to see the World's Fair in detail, as we have determined, allons à l'Exhibition."

A few hours later, as the two ladies sauntered under the gorgeous Oriental canopies known as the "India House," they came face to face with the very subject of their morning dissertation, Mr. Percy Durand.

They exchanged cordial greetings, and it seemed to Mrs. Butler that a tint as delicate as the first faint hue of dawn, colored the creamy pallor of Dolores's cheek.

"I wonder what it means?" she asked herself. "Marriage no doubt, that final Nirvana which covers so many theorists with oblivion. Heaven speed the wooing!"

At the same time Percy was thinking, "How delightful to meet a lovely and companionable girl who is entirely free to receive your polite attentions, and whom you positively know expects and desires nothing more from you. It gives a fellow such a comfortable sensation."

In view of the fact that Mr. Durand had, several times in his life, been obliged to flee from designing Mammas, and too willing maidens, we can forgive his somewhat egotistical soliloquy.

Dolores felt an agreeable sense of being perfectly at ease in the presence of Mr. Durand, and rendered herself unusually charming. Percy sauntered by the ladies while they visited various departments, and they finally lunched together. Both he and Dolores were gifted with refined wit, and ready powers of repartee, and Mrs. Butler was an appreciative listener to their gay sallies and bright criticisms.

"Positively I feel as if I had known both of you ladies all my life!" Percy said, as the day wore on. "It would require months, or years, in our own land to arrive at this pleasant feeling of comradeship. There is nothing like a rencontre in a foreign country, to break the ice of reserve."

"Quite true," Mrs. Butler responded. "We enjoy each other's society better here, too, I think, because we all indulge the vein of Bohemianism which exists in us, and which we carefully hide from view at home. For instance: I met a party of staid and respectable men and matrons from Boston the other day. They had just paid a visit to the Mabille. 'A very wicked place,' they said; 'yet everybody seems to go, so we went.' These same people would no sooner visit a concert garden in America than they would deliberately walk into Purgatory."

"I could relate similar experiences," was Percy's laughing rejoinder. "When I first came abroad I was accompanied by a very devout young man. He had often taken me to task for my Club habits. 'A fashionable club is the ante-room to a gambler's hell,' he said; and so far as I knew, he lived up to the rigorous code of morals he preached to others. What was my amazement to find his curiosity fairly unsatiable in regard to the wicked side of Parisian life.

"Beautiful parks, fine operas, and grand cathedrals and works of art, were all neglected by him, until he had explored, to his satisfaction, all the gaming-houses and variety theatres in the city of Paris. It was very amusing."

When Percy made his adieux to the ladies it was with the understanding that he should dine with them at their temporary home, on the Avenue Josephine, the following afternoon, and escort them to the theatre in the evening.

"Never before, Dolores," said Mrs. Butler, after Percy had taken his departure, "did I see you so charming as you have been to-day. Mr. Durand will be a phenomenal sort of man if he remains impervious to your charms, my dear. But then I have heard that some affair in his early life quite wrecked his heart. And so, I suppose, he has nothing but friendship to give any woman, now."

If Mrs. Butler's secret wish was to rouse the woman's desire (latent in almost every feminine heart), to strive for that which is supposed to be unattainable, it signally failed. Her remark simply gave Dolores an added sense of freedom and rest in Mr. Durand's society. "Love is like measles," she reasoned, "not liable to occur the second time."

Meanwhile Percy was saying to himself:

"She is one of the most beautiful of her sex. She pleases the eye, and entertains the mind, without touching the heart.

"Yet, it is a dangerous situation for any man to assume, this rôle of intimate friend to a lovely woman, which seems suddenly to have fallen to me. It would be wisdom on my part, and save no end of trouble, probably, if I took refuge in flight at once."

Yet what man ever fled from such sweet danger?

CHAPTER IX. JOURNALISTIC DISCUSSIONS.

Percy did not "fly" for another month, and during that time seldom a day passed that he did not spend a portion of it with Mrs. Butler and Dolores.

To the artistic rooms on the Avenue Josephine, where he was made to feel so perfectly at home, he sometimes brought a friend, and often found a bevy of bright people when he arrived.

Dolores had formed a choice circle of acquaintances among the artists, musicians, and scholars, during her prolonged sojourn abroad.

It seemed to Percy that he had never in his entire life before, met so many charming people as he encountered under Dolores's roof in that one month. There was as great a difference between the conventional society to which he had been accustomed, and the interesting clique which graced Dolores's parlors, as there is between a hotel bill of fare, and the mênu prepared for the palate of an epicure. One, monotonous insipid and flavorless; the other, spiced, appetizing and varied.

Among the score of people whom Dolores gathered together under her roof, there was a Mr. Elliott, a young English artist, a clever, cultured fellow, though something of a cockney; Monsieur Thoré, a famed historian and legislator; Madame Volkenburg, a middle-aged widow of a German professor, a lady of vast experience and wide culture, whose conversation overflowed with interesting reminiscences; and Homer Orton, an American journalist, genius and wit.

Nowhere else, in no other class or profession, can be found so much talent, and so much wit, as exists among our American journalists, however they bury the former, and misdirect the latter gift.

With a better understanding of "noblesse oblige," with a little more delicacy refining their wit, with a great deal more reverence for the sacredness of homes and personalities, to what heights might not these peerless minds elevate American journalism?

"Do you know," said Mr. Elliott, one evening in Percy's presence, addressing the journalist, "do you know, Mr. Orton, you have greatly surprised me?"

"Quite likely," responded Homer Orton, soberly gazing at his English friend. "We Americans have always been surprising you Englishmen ever since but never mind dates. I should really like to know in what especial manner I have surprised you, Mr. Elliott?"

"Well, in fact, now I beg you will not be offended, but in the fact that you are such a deuced fine fellow, you know. I had quite another impression of American newspaper men. I fancied you would not be admitted to such society as this, that you were all fellows who would sacrifice your best friends for an item, you know"

"So we would, that is, most of us," Homer interrupted, gravely. "I am a rare and beautiful exception."

"And I thought you were hardly the sort of person a lady like Miss King would want in her home, you know," the Englishman continued. "But I find you really a delightful fellow, you know, and quite a gentleman."

"Sir," said Homer, rising with his hand upon his heart, "language fails me before a compliment like this. It is a new and trying position for me to hear such words spoken of myself, and I hope you will excuse me while I walk to another part of the room and unobserved wipe away a tear of gratitude."

Then, suddenly dropping his tone of levity, the young man continued:

"But, seriously speaking, you are justified in your opinion of us as a class, Mr. Elliott, and it is to be regretted. As Mr. Durand will testify, our American eagle flaps his wings often with too much freedom."

Percy, when appealed to, was glad to express his opinion upon a subject to which he had recently given much thought.

"It is a question," he said, "which must before many years be decided, just where the freedom of the press should end and where the rights of individuals should begin. It seems to me that even our so-called best newspapers take unnecessary and unlicensed liberties in these days."

"But the public appetite demands such a varied and highly-spiced diet that we are obliged to gratify it in every legitimate manner possible. If we do not, our rival sheet will," explained Homer Orton.

"That is all very well when you keep to legitimate means. But I call the invasion of homes, and the cruel, and often untruthful, assertions concerning the private life, of unoffending individuals, illegitimate means of feeding a depraved appetite. The average newspaper humorist, who utterly disregards the truth, in his anxiety to concoct a taking item, I do not consider a necessary feature of high journalism, do you? If he only succeeds in raising a laugh, he considers his object in life attained. He reminds me of the tribe of the Damaras, who are described as so utterly heartless that they roar with laughter on beholding one of their number torn to pieces by a wild beast."

"Still it is not so much heartlessness, as insensibility and thoughtlessness, and a desire to be bright and witty, which causes a good many of these things to be written," Homer responded.

"I heard that very excuse, advanced only the other day," Percy replied, "and I heard this response made which is quite apropos now. It has been observed by thoughtful naturalists that often when a lion or a bull kills a man, the poor beast really has no malice in his heart, and does not mean any harm. He only intended to play with his accidental comrade of the moment. But then a lion has only claws and a bull only horns with which to make their humor felt, and so they are fatally misunderstood. It would seem to me, then, that the chief of a large newspaper ought to consider himself as responsible for those accidents as the keeper of a menagerie."

"But often the chief of a first-class newspaper has no idea of the really scurrilous items which creep into his paper," explained Homer. "Like the chief cook in a large hotel, he cannot taste of every dish prepared by his subordinates, and no managing editor could survive the strain, you know, of looking over his humorist's column every day. Our madhouses would overflow, if such a method of journalism were inaugurated."

"Still, it is a lax system which permits such errors (if we can call them errors) to occur," Percy insisted, "and if guests were constantly being poisoned or rendered ill through the criminal carelessness of the hotel cook, I fancy he would be called to account for not knowing what dishes his subordinates prepared. A newspaper should be the friend and companion of the people, and a welcome guest in every home. Instead, it is too often a treacherous spy, a maligner and falsifier. Almost every day we read statements concerning people, which are absolutely without foundation, and which result in no end of mischief and trouble."

"You no doubt refer to people in public life, politicians, authors, actors, and the like, do you not?" asked Homer. "I know they are considered targets for the shots of our humorists all over the country, but then you must remember that if a man gives his name voluntarily to the world, and forces his work or his personality upon the public, that he cannot expect both the benefits of fame and the seclusion of private life. It is unreasonable. He has in a measure given himself over to the public, and he must take the consequences. And, really, the fact that the busy newspapers of the present day give time and space to discussion or comments upon any individual ought to be considered highly complimentary."

"That depends entirely upon the nature of the comments," answered Percy. "Nor do I refer entirely to public people. Our wealthy men, and their wives and daughters, are subjected to the same coarse comments. Their personal defects are ridiculed, and the pitiless and ghastly electric light of publicity is turned on their most sacred joys or sorrows. Items devoid of truth and wit, appear every day concerning people who have committed no offense greater than to succeed in some special calling. They are copied, enlarged upon, and believed by a majority of the masses. It is a degenerate system of journalism which permits it. It is high time some manly journalist began a crusade against it."

"I agree with you, perfectly," Homer Orton answered. "I would like to have the leading newspapers of the country band together to protect the people from insult and petty libels in their columns: and I would like to see the Imaginary Interviewer done away with by every respectable journal."

"What is the Imaginary Interviewer, pray?" queried the Englishman.

"He is a reporter, who, if he is refused admittance by any person he wishes to interview, deliberately invents an interview; describes the personality and manufactures the conversation to suit his own taste. No one was ever more misused in this respect than your own Oscar Wilde, unless it was Mrs. Langtry. The most astounding postures and inane remarks were attributed to them by people who never saw them. It is not, however, our first-class journals which have permitted this."

"Would you not recommend the abolishing of the interviewer entirely?" suggested Percy.

"Certainly not," Homer responded. "The newspaper interviewer is a benefit to the press, to the country, and to all public people who have a name and a reputation to make. That is, when he is a truthful gentleman, and does not abuse the hospitality of those who admit him to their homes."

"The school-girl who sends for the autograph of a public man pays him a graceful compliment, and he should write it for her without a murmur."

"Just in the same way, the whole public offers a quiet ovation to the man of reputation when an interviewer presents his card. The newspaper would never ask for an interview to publish, unless the masses of its readers desired it. And the interviewer should be met courteously, and the public man should realize that this sort of thing is the duty he pays on fame. If he has positively nothing of interest to say to the interviewer, or is too busily engaged to be interrupted, he should tell the caller so in a respectful and polite manner. Many a public man is badly treated by the reporter in print, because he treated the reporter badly in his house."

"But what have you to say of the interviewer who is well treated, and then repays the hospitality he has received by an article bristling with ridicule and untruthful misrepresentations of the personality or conversation of his entertainer? I have known this to occur."

"I do not believe it occurs very often," Homer answered. "When it does, there is usually personal malice at the bottom of it, or a catering to the lowest order of scurrilous journalism. It is a great pity that the victims in such cases have no dignified redress. A thorough caning ought to be considered consistent with the situation. But, I think, as a rule, respectable newspaper men endeavor to do the right thing by those who have treated them with courtesy in this matter. The trouble is, journals are not careful enough in the representatives they send on these commissions. It requires a great deal of delicate tact to write acceptably of a man's home-life and personality during his life-time. No thoughtless boy, or sensation-seeking reporter, should be commissioned with such a task. I positively know a New York journalist, who possesses a bright mind and wonderful command of language beside an easy and elegant deportment, who considers it fair play to gain information through private letters or confidential conversations with his friends, and then to use such knowledge for press purposes. He boasts of his skill in this respect."

"Impossible!" cried Percy, indignantly.

"Quite too possible," Homer replied. "His devotion to journalism, and his desire to feed the public appetite, has destroyed every particle of moral principle the fellow ever possessed. Of course, such a man reflects discredit upon the whole profession. That he is an exception to the rule, I know, but that he is retained at all upon a respectable journal, is to be regretted."

"There is still another feature of American journalism to be more regretted and blushed for, I think," said Percy. "That is, the attitude of our so called humorists and paragraphers toward public women. No where else in the world do women occupy so exalted and honored a position as they occupy in America. No other women in the world have accomplished so much in various public callings. Yet no where else are they subjected to such insults as they receive from the newspapers throughout the United States, from the prima donna to the President's wife, sister, or daughter."

"Are you not a little extreme in that statement, Mr. Durand?" asked Homer Orton. "You must recollect that the royal family are discussed very freely in print, and ladies who have become famous ought to consider themselves members of the royal family of Genius, and take newspaper criticisms as a natural consequence."

"It is not newspaper criticisms to which I refer," answered Percy. "Of course, half the success of an actress, a singer, an author or a painter depends upon public criticism, and often it happens that the severer the criticisms the greater the success. But it is the loose familiarity and the coarse jests of the item-seeker of which I speak. Only last week I saw a wretched little item, intended to be humorous, but actually brutal, going the rounds of the press, concerning the advanced years of a famous opera singer, a woman who has reflected credit on our nation by her brilliant and stainless career."

"I saw the item to which you refer," Mr. Elliott said, "and I wondered if it was consistent with the National boast that Americans are the kindest and most thoughtful men in the world toward ladies. It seemed to me an uncalled-for and ungentlemanly incivility toward a noble lady."

"I often wonder," continued Percy, "if the fellows who perpetrate those things stop and consider that the public women, whose names they use so freely, are somebody's sisters, wives, or mothers, and that, in nine cases out of ten, they lead a public life, or first entered a public career, to earn a living. If the newspaper men of the country ever do take this view of the matter, I should think their first impulse would be to shield and protect and help every self-supporting woman in the land. At all events, I should think every sensible journalist would realize that, while it is the province of the newspaper to furnish able criticism on the voice of the singer, the book of the author, the speech of the orator, it is not its province to indulge in poor puns, or insulting comments on the age, the personal defects, or the domestic life of the singer, author or speaker. These things should be tabooed by respectable journals, just as they are tabooed in respectable society. Our journalists should be as careful, in their references to the private matters of individuals in print, as they are in conversation in their parlors, where scandalous or impertinent references to the absent would be considered 'bad form.' Really, I do not understand how any of us who read the daily papers dare boast of American chivalry."

"The chivalry of the average man," said Dolores, who approached the group just at this moment, "consists in protecting a woman against every man save himself. And now, gentlemen, we are to have a recitation from Madame Volkenburg. Will you join us and listen?"

CHAPTER X. A DISCOURSE ON SUICIDE

One day Mrs. Butler, Dolores, Percy, and several of their friends went to visit the Latin Quarter, the ancient homes of the Grisettes, a race rapidly becoming extinct.

"I have always wanted to visit this locality," Dolores said on her way thither. "It is a phase of Parisian life which has possessed a curious fascination for me."

"No doubt you have surrounded the Grisettes with a halo of romance," answered Percy. "If so, it will vanish utterly as you approach. What sort of beings do you fancy they are?"

"Physically, lovely sirens: mentally frivolous; morally lax, owing to their education, no doubt. Just the style of woman to fascinate a romantic student."

Percy laughed. "That is the prevailing idea," he said; "but it is wholly unlike the reality, as you will see."

What Dolores saw, were groups of contented looking mothers, tidy housewives, and comfortable young matrons. Women whose lives were devoted to their homes and families. Universally neat, and modest in appearance, but in no case strikingly attractive or beautiful.

"There is every indication here of happy domestic life," Percy said. "These women make good true consorts, and contented companions. They exchange their culinary and housekeeping accomplishments, and their loyalty, for a little affection, protection and support. On the whole, they lead a very pleasant sort of existence, while it lasts."

"Their position is far more enviable than that of the average wife," Dolores responded, "for if they are unhappy in their relations, they can at least get away; and I have no doubt they receive more devotion and loyalty than the majority of married women do. The position of the latter seems to me the more humiliating of the two."

Percy regarded Dolores with a grave expression.

"You are a strange girl," he said. "Yet extreme as you are in your ideas, there is much truth in what you say. I have very little respect for the husbands of my acquaintance. And still I believe God meant each man to possess one mate, and to be true to her in life and death. That is my ideal of perfect manhood, though an ideal I never expect to attain. There was a time when I imagined it possible, but now I live for the pleasure of the hour, and waste no time in theories or in moralizing. Life is too short. But of one thing I am sure, Miss King, positively sure." He paused, and she looked up expecting some serious remark. "And that is, that you are the most charming companion in the world."

On their way back to the Avenue Josephine, they saw a beautiful girl who had just shot herself in the breast, being conveyed to the hospital. Her lovely features were distorted with pain, and her agonizing groans, as they lifted her from the street where she had fallen, were heartrending to hear. Later, as they sat in Dolores' parlors, they all fell to discussing suicide.

"Terrible as it may seem," Dolores said, "I really cannot think it so great a crime as many do. We are never consulted in regard to coming into this world. Life is thrust upon us, and if, as in the case of that poor girl, perhaps, it becomes an insupportable burden, I cannot help thinking God will forgive the suffering soul that lays the burden down. I have always felt the greatest sympathy for suicides. It is a cowardly act, I own, yet it is a cowardice I can comprehend and condone. And I think God will surely be as sympathetic as a mortal."

"You know Dante's description of the Seventh Circle," suggested Percy, "and the horrors which await the rash soul of a suicide:

"When departs the fierce soul from the body, by itself Thence torn asunder, to the seventh Gulf By Minos doomed, into the wood it falls, No place assigned, but where so ever Chance hurled it."

"But that was merely the poetic utterance of a visionary mind," Dolores answered. "No one in these days believes in a God who could be guilty of such atrocious punishments for sin or error, as Dante describes; and then I contend that in many instances suicide is not a crime, it is merely a cowardly act."

"But laying aside the crime of the act, think what an uncomfortable position the poor soul may find itself in!" suggested Percy. "To go where we are not wanted or invited, in this world, is a very embarrassing situation, you know. And to suddenly thrust yourself, without an invitation, upon the exclusive society of angels, I must say I would not have the courage to do it."

"Well, of all things," said Madam Volkenburg, "if any of you ever do commit suicide, never shoot yourselves, or resort to any disgusting or painful process. I can tell you of a very swift and painless method."

"What is it?" they all asked, in chorus, fascinated, as most of us always are, by a discussion of the horrible.

All but Dolores. She already knew.

"Oh, it is a swift poison," Madam Volkenburg explained. "My husband, who was a great experimenter in the chemical world, as you perhaps know, left a package of it among his possessions. It is a white, brilliant, crystallized substance, and the smallest particle of it, the moment it mixes with the saliva of the mouth, and is swallowed, produces instant death, and there is nothing to indicate poison afterward. It cannot be detected, and it leaves the body quietly composed as if sudden sleep had overtaken it."

"Why is it not better known?" some one asked.

"Perhaps it is well known; perhaps many of the sudden deaths by 'heart disease,' of which we read so often, occur in this way."

"And it will produce, as Madame Volkenburg says, swift and painless death, at least upon an animal," added Dolores. "When my little dog was run over by a carriage wheel, and lay crying in terrible pain, and I knew he must die, I tested the efficacy of this poison upon him. It ended his agonies instantly."

"And by the way," spoke Madame laughingly, turning to Dolores, "I gave you enough of the poison to kill ten dogs, or human beings, either; and you never returned it to me. Since I have heard your views upon suicide I think I had better take the dangerous drug out of your possession."

"If I were anxious to die, I fancy the absence of that drug would not prevent me from finding the means of self-destruction," Dolores answered, lightly. And at that moment refreshments were served, and the conversation turned upon more agreeable subjects.

At the expiration of a month, the swiftest month of his life, it seemed to Percy, he was obliged to cut loose from this pleasant circle, and visit London and Berlin, on the business which had really brought him abroad.

He felt a curious depression of spirits as he entered the parlors on the Avenue Josephine the evening preceding his departure, a depression which he was hardly able to explain to himself. Only this might be his last interview with his charming friends, and "last times" are always sad.

Dolores seemed grave, as she welcomed him, and a little later she said, with a winning frankness, "I never remember to have felt so lonely at the thought of any other person's departure in my life, Mr. Durand, as I feel at yours. You have been such an addition to our circle; you are such a bon comrade; just what a brother would be, I fancy. How I shall miss you!"

"But I am not your brother, you know," Percy said, and he wanted to add, "And therefore the association has its dangers." He left it unsaid, however, thinking she would understand his simple assertion.

But she did not. She was a woman with a hobby, which precluded the thought of marriage. And she was a cold woman by nature. Knowing that Mr. Durand fully understood and respected her views, she could see no danger in his companionship. She was very lonely at the thought of his departure. He was her ideal friend, lost as soon as found.

"It has been a charming month in Bohemia," Percy continued. "I have thoroughly enjoyed it, it is unlike anything I have ever experienced before. I have had my fill of conventional society, and I have drained the cup of reckless pleasures; but this charming mixture of refinement, esprit and abandon, has been a new element to me."

"Apropos to your reference to a month in Bohemia," said Dolores, "I believe Mr. Orton has written a poem on Bohemia, which he has kindly promised to deliver this evening. Mr. Orton, will you favor us now?"

"I was not aware that you were a poet, Mr. Orton," Percy remarked, as the young man arose, and began to affect the bashful-school-girl air.

"Sir," said the journalist, turning a stern look upon Percy, and speaking in a sepulchral tone, "I am all that is bad: a newspaper man, a poet, and" pointing toward the piano, "the worst remains to be told; I am a pianist." And then, quickly changing his expression and voice, he recited in the most admirable manner the following verses:

BOHEMIA.

Bohemia, o'er thy unatlassed borders How many cross, with half-reluctant feet, And unformed fears of dangers and disorders. To find delights, more wholesome and more sweet Than ever yet were known to the "elite."

Herein can dwell no pretence and no seeming; No stilted pride thrives in this atmosphere, Which stimulates a tendency to dreaming. The shores of the ideal world, from here, Seem sometimes to be tangible and near.

We have no use for formal codes of fashion; No "Etiquette of Courts" we emulate; We know it needs sincerity and passion To carry out the plans of God, or fate; We do not strive to seem inanimate.

We call no time lost that we give to pleasure; Life's hurrying river speeds to Death's great sea; We cast out no vain plummet-line to measure Imagined depths of that unknown To Be, But grasp the Now, and fill it full of glee.

All creeds have room here, and we all together Devoutly worship at Art's sacred shrine; But he who dwells once in thy golden weather, Bohemia, sweet, lovely land of mine. Can find no joy outside thy border-line.

"That is just the fear which disturbs my heart, as I am about to cross the border-line and go back to the common-place world," sighed Percy, when the applause which succeeded the recitation died away. "I doubt my ability to enjoy anything, after this delightful experience."

"Well, now," said Homer Orton, "in response to the encore I ought to have received, I will give you a few verses appropriate to that situation, my dear fellow. If you commit them to memory, they may serve to help you in those dark hours of mental and spiritual pain which come to every man, the morning after the club supper. They are called

PENALTY.

Because of the fullness of what I had, All that I have seems poor and vain. If I had not been happy, I were not sad, Tho' my salt is savorless, why complain?

From the ripe perfection of what was mine, All that is mine seems worse than naught; Yet I know, as I sit in the dark, and pine, No cup could be drained which had not been fraught.

From the throb and thrill of a day that was, The day that now is seems dull with gloom; Yet I bear the dullness and darkness, because 'Tis but the reaction of glow and bloom.

From the royal feast that of old was spread, I am starved on the diet that now is mine; Yet, I could not turn hungry from water and bread, If I had not been sated on fruit and wine."

"Speaking of Bohemia," Dolores said, "with all its charms, I do not believe I am a Bohemian by nature. I am really fond of ceremonies and imposing forms. I enjoy the most impressive services in divine worship. Had I been reared in the Roman Church, I would have made one of its most devout members. I like conventional life, but I do not like the people I meet in those circles."

"And yet," Percy answered, "it is generally supposed that in exclusive circles one finds all that is choice."

"But it is a great mistake," continued Dolores. "It may be true that whatever is choice is always exclusive; but whatever is exclusive is not always choice. One finds so little variety in the people one meets in the so-called best society anywhere. They are all after one pattern, and society does not tolerate individual tastes and ideas, you know. So you see I am obliged to select my congenial friends as I may, and create a Bohemia of my own."

"Which immediately becomes a Paradise," her listener answered gallantly.

"Don't," ejaculated Dolores with a pained expression, "it sounds so like, well, so like other men."

"And am I not like other men?" Percy asked, smiling and secretly pleased. Nothing flatters a man's vanity more than being told he is not like other men. "I never imagined myself to be a distinct type."

"But you are; or at least you have seemed so to me. And that is why I have liked you so well."

"Then you do like me?"

Dolores met his gaze without a blush or tremor, frankly, sweetly.

"I do not think I ever met any man before, whom I so thoroughly liked and respected," she said. "You are my ideal friend."

"Then, perhaps you will consent to correspond with me occasionally," Percy suggested. "I should have gone away not daring to ask the favor, believing myself only one of the many on whom you bestowed your hospitality, but for your kind speech."

As he sat in his room that night, Percy puzzled his brains, trying to analyze Dolores King's manner and words, and state of mind toward him.

"She is either the most perfect actress, or the coldest and most passionless woman on earth," he said, "incapable of any strong emotion. Or else, or else, she likes me better than she knows. At all events, it is fortunate for both, that I am going away."

CHAPTER XI. A FREAK OF FATE

Percy, who had long believed himself to be a perfect cosmopolitan, quite as much at home in one part of the globe as in another, was surprised to find that he was actually homesick after leaving Paris.

With an impatience he could hardly understand, he awaited Dolores' response to his first letter. When it came, full of bright humor and sparkling cynicism, pleasant gossip and sincere expressions of regret at his absence, Percy sat and smoked, and dreamed over it for more than an hour.

He was trying to analyze his own feelings. When a woman does this, ten to one she is in love. When a man does it, ten to one he is not.

Percy did not believe himself to be in love.

"At least," he mused, "I could never, even were I a marrying man, contemplate marriage with Dolores King. She is too cold, too caustic, too skeptical. In fact, she understands human nature too well. I should want a wife who would idolize me, who would set me up as a hero, to worship. I think many a man becomes a hero, through having some woman over-estimate his worth. Rather than disillusion her, he acquires the qualities with which her loving imagination has invested him. Many a man has been saved from yielding to temptation at the last moment, because he could not shatter the perfect faith of some trusting heart. Dolores would not surround a man with any halo. She sees us all as we are, perhaps exaggerating our defects somewhat. She would suspect a man of evil on the slightest provocation, and that is the surest way to drive a human being into wrongdoing.

"But she is a delightful comrade, and so exquisitely beautiful that the plainest room would seem elegantly furnished if she occupied it.

"She understands the art of entertaining. And time hangs heavy on a fellow's hands, after he has lost her society. After all, life is too short to relinquish any pleasure within our grasp, for fear of consequences." And, rising and tossing aside his cigar, he added aloud:

"With the Persian poet I can say,

"O threats of Hell, and hopes of Paradise, One thing at least is certain, this life flies. One thing is certain, and the rest is lies. The flower that once has blown forever dies."

A few weeks later, Percy received letters from New York, requesting him to visit London, there to complete business arrangements with a large export house, and then to proceed to Copenhagen, where it would be necessary for him to remain several months in the interest of the firm.

When the letter arrived, he had just dispatched one to Dolores, which closed as follows:

"I expect to return to America next month. I go with regret, and yet no doubt it is for the best. It will cut short our delightful yet dangerous companionship, but I trust you will permit me to call upon you and say farewell before I go. In your last, you mentioned the possibility of leaving Paris soon, but you did not tell me what your plans were. Wherever you are, I shall, with your permission, find you, before I sail for America."

What was his astonishment to receive in reply to his letter, the information that Dolores, accompanied by Mrs. Butler and Madame Volkenburg were about to start on a journey to the Land of the Midnight Sun.

"We go direct to Moscow first," wrote Dolores, "stopping there long enough to drop a tear on the tombs of the Czars; then on to St. Petersburg; then by steamer down the Gulf of Finland and across the Baltic to Stockholm; thence by rail to Christiania, where we may linger some time, as Madame Volkenburg has dear friends there. From Christiania we go direct to the North Cape. It is our intention to return via Copenhagen and the Channels, as late in the season as we can safely make the trip. We do not leave Paris under three weeks; I hope you will call upon us before your return to America, as you have promised."

When Percy read this he laughed aloud.

"It is fate," he said. "We are destined to be thrown together. I shall proceed at once to Copenhagen, and when my charming friends arrive in Christiania, I shall join them there and make the journey with them to the North Cape."

It needed this bright prospect to keep Percy's heart cheerful after he arrived in Copenhagen. Not a person in the city had hung out a sign of furnished rooms to let; so finally he decided to advertise. After waiting two days for the advertisement to appear, he rushed off to the printing office to demand an explanation. The clerk remarked calmly, that it had been lost, and as the next day was Sunday, he would be obliged to wait until Monday. On Monday the notice appeared, badly printed, in a column headed "Servant Girls Wanted."

During that day Percy found a room to his liking, on the Tordenskjoldsgade, but as he feared an attack of lockjaw if he attempted to direct any one to his lodgings, he chose apartments on the Hovedvagtsgade instead. His breakfast, when served, consisted of a cup of coffee and a cold roll. His dinner, for which he had a ravenous appetite, was better enjoyed in anticipation than participation. The soup was devoid of any extract of flesh, fish, or fowl, but contained quantities of ginger, citron, lemon, and sugar. This was followed by boiled fish, tasteless and watery, and cauliflower swimming in sauce composed of milk and black pepper. There were no side-dishes, and the eagerly-expected dessert brought only disappointment and bread and cheese.

The next day, Percy was so curious concerning a mysterious plate of soup which was served, that he made inquiries and learned the actual ingredients. They consisted of carrots, potatoes, cabbage, sugar, eels, cinnamon, cherries, plums, and small pieces of pork. Another soup was made from the first milk of a cow; and what was known as "beer soup," flavored with various ingredients, was frequently served.

On inquiry, Percy found that other boarding-houses and hotels furnished the same mênu, and he could only better his condition by boarding at the largest hotel at an exorbitant price. Finally he became reconciled to the fare: esteemed Limburger cheese as a delicacy, and hailed the advent of every new kind of soup, as he wrote home to his cousin, "with all the enthusiasm of a scientific explorer."

His next achievement was learning how to sleep in a Danish bed. The cot was so narrow, and so rounded in the middle, that if he forgot himself and fell asleep, the covers were sure to slide off one side or the other; and any effort to detain them resulted in his own downfall. Finally, he concluded to lie under the feather bed, instead of over it; and thus, braced by the wall on one side and two chairs on the other, and the huge tick settling down over him, he succeeded in wooing slumber.

After two months devoted to business in Copenhagen, he took passage one autumn afternoon, in the steamship "Aarhus," for Christiania, where he was to join Dolores and her party. Passing through the "Kattegat," a severe wind rendered most of his companions seasick, and Percy was almost the only one who escaped the infliction. The next morning, one of the passengers asked the captain if the storm had been a severe one. For answer he simply pointed to the smoke-stack, which was encrusted to its very summit with the salt from the waves which had dashed over it in the night.

Percy stopped at the beautiful city of Gottenburg for a day, and made a journey into the Northwest some fifty miles to visit the famous falls of Trollhatton, which are unsurpassed in all Europe. In a letter to his cousin that night he wrote as follows:

"On the little cluster of houses, which constitute the village of Trollhatton, I was surprised to see in bold letters the name of a New York sewing-machine company. I had seen the sign in France and Germany, but I hardly expected to find it in this wild, unsettled portion of Sweden. The same day, in traversing the vast, dreary, rocky plateau which stretches from Lake Venern to the Skagerak, a large, freshly-painted sign of 'Fairbank Scales' met my eye. But in fact, where you find anything good over here in the way of machinery, you may be sure it is from America.

"In all my travels through Germany I have never seen a reaper, a mower, or a steel plow. Most of the grain seemed to be cut with a sickle. In a very few instances I saw men using an awkward sort of cradle; but they always threw their swath into the standing grain instead of away from it, and had women follow behind with sickles to pick it out and lay it in shape, so I did not see that they gained much.

"It may be true that the American is somewhat given to bragging; but when he comes to see the clumsy old-fashioned way of doing things in Europe, and compares it with the methods at home, he begins to feel that he has a foundation for his boasting. The best fire-arms, the best cutlery, the best furniture, and the best tools, all come from America. Even American cheese has found its way all over Europe, and our various brands of tobacco are as familiar to the European smoker, as to the Yankee himself."

Two days later found Percy enjoying a delightful interview with his friends in Christiania; and the next day the happy quartette started on their journey to the Land of the Midnight Sun.

CHAPTER XII. AN EXCITING ICE-BOAT ADVENTURE

During six delightful weeks of travel and sightseeing through the wonderfully picturesque scenery of Sweden and Norway, Percy was again the comrade and escort of Dolores.

Day by day a thousand nameless acts of kindness and respectful unobtrusive attentions, as thoughtful as they were delicate, endeared him to the heart, at whose portal love, clothed in his most ancient and most successful disguise of friendship, was effecting an entrance.

It was late in November when the party returned to Copenhagen.

"My business matters will detain me here a week, possibly ten days," Percy said. "You will need that time to thoroughly enjoy the Thorvaldsen and the Ethnological Museums, which are in their way the finest in the world. Then I shall be ready to escort you to Paris, before I report myself at London."

Madame Volkenburg returned to Christiania the day previous to the intended departure of her friends. But at the expiration of the week, just as Percy was planning to make an exit from the cold bleak Island, Dolores sprained her ankle, and was unable to leave her room during four weeks. Percy found business enough to employ a few hours of each day in the interest of the London and American houses, and the remainder of the time he passed agreeably in entertaining the ladies. He read aloud, told interesting stories of adventure and travel, and made himself so thoroughly charming that Dolores forgot her misfortune in view of the happy hours it brought her.

When she at length declared herself able to proceed upon her journey another obstacle presented itself. The weather became unusually cold; and the Sounds, surrounding the island on which Copenhagen is situated, were packed with jagged blocks of ice, too thick to be broken by a steamer, but not sufficiently connected to make it safe for men or teams to venture on them. Our friends were prisoners, consequently, upon an almost inaccessible island.

"The blockade cannot last forever," Percy said, when he had informed the ladies of the condition of matters. "That is all the consolation I can give you at present. It may last a week, or a month, I am led to understand. In the meantime, we must enjoy ourselves as best we can. I am very sorry Madame Volkenburg did not remain with us, to share a little jaunt to Kaskilde, the ancient Capital of Denmark, which we will make to-morrow."

"What is there to see at Kaskilde?" inquired Dolores.

"A cathedral, of course," Percy answered. "No doubt you are tired of cathedrals, but this is a famous one: a relic of the ancient grandeur of the city when it numbered 100,000 souls. Its population is less than 5,000 now. You will find much to interest you there, as this building has been the burial-place of nearly all the Danish kings."

Kaskilde was not more than twenty miles from Copenhagen, and accessible by rail.

Dolores was surprised to find many of the tombs exquisitely carved with marble and alabaster. One of the most interesting bore the life-sized figure of Queen Margaret, who died in 1412. The beautifully-portrayed features, full of expression, were declared to be a correct likeness of the fair queen.

In the centre of the church upon a large iron slab set into the floor, it was recorded that "This spot is purchased by Nils Jurgersen, of the Church, as a resting place for his posterity for all time to come: in order that his family need not change their burial-place every twenty years, as other people do." But in spite of this sarcastic reference to other people, the royal mandate went forth, that no more people not of royal blood should be buried in the church. And Nils Jurgersen's descendants are obliged to sleep out of doors, like "other people," after all.

High up in the nave of the church stood a huge clock. Before it two half-sized figures carved in wood. At the end of each hour, the man struck the time with a hammer upon the face of the clock: while the quarter-hours were struck by the woman against a small bell.

"This little old couple have been faithful to each other during four hundred years," said Percy, as he stood beside Dolores watching the figures. "Is not that a wonderful illustration of constancy?"

"Yes," Dolores answered, laughing. "Such illustrations are readily found, in wood. But how presumptive of man, to produce such an example, when the Creator gave him no human precedent!"

"I must tell you about the clock," continued Percy. "Originally, there were figures of St. George upon a horse, fighting the Dragon. Every time the clock struck, the Dragon sprang upon the horse, and the latter gave a wild scream. But there was an old priest who complained that the noise of this battle disturbed him in his preaching: so the Knight and the Dragon, wonderful pieces of mechanism, were destroyed to please one conceited old egotist. And, furthermore, he commanded that the faithful old couple should be compelled to keep the Sabbath like other people. The machinery of the clock was so arranged, in accordance with his wishes, that no hours have been struck on the Sabbath since that time."

Hanging in a prominent part of the church, Mrs. Butler discovered a painting which amused her greatly. It represented the devil, well horned and hoofed, gazing sharply at the pews, in his hand a pencil and a scroll. On the latter was inscribed: "I make a note of all those who come late or go around and tattle."

"I wish I were able to purchase this painting and send it over to America," Mrs. Butler remarked. "We need it there, I am sure."

At the expiration of two weeks, the blockade still continued. The whole Baltic, as well as the North Sea, was one mass of floating ice, which the powerful currents and tides in the connecting channels kept in motion.

If the reader has not visited this portion of Europe, by glancing at any map he will see that the Northwestern part of Denmark consists of two islands. The Western is known as Funem, the Eastern as Zealand.

The "Great Belt," as the channel between them is called, is from fifteen to twenty miles wide in the narrowest portion, and is so called to distinguish it from the channel between Funem and the mainland, known as the "Little Belt."

In ordinary years, these straits remain sufficiently open, so that steamers can cross regularly; or else they freeze solidly, allowing sleighs to transfer freight and passengers.

But now, Copenhagen was entirely cut off from all communication with the outside world.

Percy was told, however, that an effort was being made to carry the mails across the Sound in a sort of ice-boat.

On investigation, he discovered that these ice-boats were in fact large, strongly-built fishing-smacks, with iron runners on the bottom. Each boat carried a crew of eight or ten weather-beaten old fishermen.

"If you can convey the mails across the Channel in those boats, why can't you carry passengers?" Percy asked as he stood inspecting the smacks the day before their intended venture.

The men laughed, and gave him to understand in broken German, the language he had used, that any man could go who had the courage to make the attempt.

As he related this to Mrs. Butler and Dolores a little later, he said: "If I had the least idea when navigation would open and permit you to make your escape, I would go on the ice-boat to-morrow. Business cares begin to weigh upon me heavily. But I do not like to leave you imprisoned here for an indefinite time."

"Why could not we, too, go by the ice-boat?" suggested Dolores.

"Impossible!" cried Percy, aghast.

"By no means. We are experienced travelers, and the adventure would be exhilarating after our long imprisonment here. If the crew are opposed, I will go myself and talk them into consenting."

"Although they could not understand a word you speak, I know you would win their consent to anything," laughed Percy. "But I will see if the plan is practicable."

An hour later, he returned from a second interview with the ice-boat crew.

"You can go," he said, "if your courage will sustain you. Reduce your hand luggage to the smallest possible compass, and be prepared to start for Korsör this P. M. at five o'clock. We remain there over night. We take passage in the boat early in the morning. Two other gentlemen are to accompany us, so we shall not die alone."

In the chilly dawn of the following morning our little party stood wondering where they were to be stored in those queer-looking smacks, one loaded with the heavier baggage, the other half-filled with mail bags. The ladies were soon told to take seats in the rear boat, among the mail bags; while the men were instructed to run alongside, and to be prepared to spring into it at a moment's notice. The crew pulled on a long rope attached to the prow of the boat, and it gave a lurch forward.

For thirty or forty rods from shore, the ice was solid, and slanted down toward the water. The boats glided along easily and rapidly. The ladies laughed gleefully and enjoyed the novel mode of locomotion.

All the crew, and the three gentlemen passengers, were provided with huge straw overshoes, the soles fully two inches thick. These served to protect their feet from the cold, and prevented slipping on the ice.

"What rare good sport!" cried Dolores, looking like a Russian princess in her furs, as she smiled up into Percy's face, while he ran lightly along beside her.

"It is like the coasting days of childhood on a large scale."

Just then there came an ominous cracking sound, and suddenly the forward boat crashed through the ice, which gave way for rods in every direction. The rear boat went shooting down an inclined plane into the water. The ladies shrieked, the crew shouted, the boat turned over on its side, but was speedily righted.

Percy succeeded in springing into the boat before it reached the open sea, but the other two passengers clung to its side, their legs dangling in the icy water.

The forward crew threw out a long rope and a plank, and, getting out on the ice, pulled the boat along a few lengths. The rear boat was pushed along in its wake through the broken ice. As they proceeded farther from the shore, the ice became more uneven. Where it was strong, the crew propelled the boats by means of the ropes; but where it was shaky or broken, the oars and boards were brought into requisition. The old seamen found constant amusement in the terrified screams of Mrs. Butler, every time they crashed through the ice, while Dolores seemed to enjoy the excitement with an almost childish delight.

Upon a sort of sand-bar in one place, which marked the boundary between the fixed or land-ice, and the loose cakes floating in the Sound, immense blocks had been crowded into all sorts of fantastic shapes, forming an irregular rampart thirty or forty feet high.

Beyond this, the crew was able to keep the boat in the water most of the time, winding in and out among the islands of ice.

Once, they were caught in a narrow strip of water between two ice-floes.

Then the crew became excited, and hurriedly ran the boat up on the ice out of harm's way. A few minutes later, the edges of the ice-floes began to grind together and double up, impelled by the tremendous currents underneath.

Dolores, who had grown very pale, while they were in this perilous situation, shivered slightly, as she heard the grinding of the ice-floes, and suddenly swayed back unconscious.

Percy reached out his arm just in time to receive her inanimate form.

The swoon lasted but a moment: yet during that moment Percy experienced the delicious pleasure of holding her fair head upon his shoulder, of clasping her lovely shape against his heart. All his well-controlled emotions seemed to cry out against their long constraint; and a sudden desire to seize her in his arms and cover her beautiful face with kisses might have overruled his reason, his sense of propriety and his good breeding, had she not opened her eyes and drawn herself out of his arms.

"How foolish I am," she said. "But I really thought we were to be crushed between those great ice jaws. I will not be so weak again."

"Please do," whispered Percy. "It was the happiest moment of my life." His warm audible breath fanned her cheek; his eyes were full of a fire she had never before seen in them; her blood tingled through her veins, producing a slight intoxication. Her lids drooped, her cheek crimsoned, but she did not rebuke him for his speech or his glance.

A strange, sweet languor filled her heart, and rendered any commonplace remark impossible. For the first time in her life she was conscious of a vague pleasure in the close proximity of a human being.

Out in the middle of the Sound they could see the black smoke of the steamer "Absolem" awaiting them in a long strip of open sea. By noon they were within a mile of her: and here the crew stopped their boats in the middle of an ice-floe, and served a sort of Arctic dinner.

An hour later, they reached the steamer; the mails and passengers were transferred and the ice-boats returned to Korsör.

The "Absolem" had been two days and two nights in the ice, and had narrowly escaped destruction among the sunken rocks, whither it had been carried by the powerful ice currents.

But now, with an open sea before them, they approached the western shore. As they neared Nyborg, Percy called the attention of the ladies to the remarkable thickness of the land ice. And to their surprise a few moments later, they saw the ship make fast to this clearly-defined and solid ice pier, and unload its freight and passengers as readily as if it had been in harbor.

Here they were huddled into Russian sleighs, and driven rapidly to the station at Nyborg, where they took the train for Hamburg.

CHAPTER XIII. A STAR FALLS

Percy found letters in London, which gave him the opportunity of remaining in Europe permanently, if he chose to accept it. The business outlook was fine, and the position most desirable for him. Yet he decided to refuse it; to return to America at once, and send someone else to fill the vacancy. A farewell letter he wrote to Dolores will explain his reasons. It read as follows:

"MY DEAR MISS KING:

"I have decided, somewhat suddenly, to return to America, despite the fact that my senior partners desire me to accept a permanent position abroad.

"I shall sail next week and without seeing you again. I hope you will not think me discourteous.

"But to be frank, Miss Dolores, I find our intimate acquaintance growing constantly more dangerous. I am not a marrying man, as you know; and I respect your views on the same subject. Even if I wished I could not change those views; and no greater mistake could be made by two people who entertained our ideas, than to permit any combination of circumstances to bind them together for life. Yet, at the same time, it is impossible for two young unmarried persons like ourselves, neither of us owing allegiance to any third party, to continue long in this fraternal sort of comradeship, which now exists, between us. You are a beautiful and fascinating woman. I am by no means a second Plato. In spite of my wish to please you, and to be the perfect friend you are so kind as to call me, I find myself constantly irritated with your calm, emotionless demeanor toward me. I would not offend you by any word of love; yet I am obliged to be always on my guard when in your presence, and when I am absent from you, I feel a feverish desire to be near you. Your beauty and your brightness and your many agreeable qualities are an aggravation to me. I am aware that it is something more (or less) than a feeling of friendship which has taken possession of me, and, since it is so, the only wise course lies in flight. For,

He who loves and runs away May live to love another day.

I shall always be your friend, and I hope you will continue to answer my letters. You have been a revelation to me in many ways, and my experience in your society can never be forgotten. I am sure I am better for it. Yet I am only mortal, and I can but be rendered unhappy by a continuation of what has been so pleasant. La Bruyéré was right when he said, that friendship was impossible between the sexes. I beg you to forgive the extreme frankness of this letter, and to think of me as your weak, selfish, yet

"Admiring friend, "PERCY DURAND."

He sealed and addressed the letter, and rang for a boy to post it. But at that moment a rap sounded at his door, and a telegram was placed in his hands. He tore it open and read:

PARIS, FRANCE.

"Mrs. Butler is dying; will you come to me?

"DOLORES."

Aside from the sorrow he felt at the news of Mrs. Butler's illness, Percy read the telegram with an actual sense of relief. We all remember to have experienced the feeling at some time in our lives, when inclination warred with conscience, and Fate, constituting herself umpire, decided in favor of inclination.

"There is no escaping Destiny. After all, whatever the Power that rules this world, we are

"Impotent pieces of the game he plays, Upon the checker-board of nights and days,"

he said, as he placed the letter he had written in his pocket, and scribbled a hasty reply to Dolores' telegram.

Arriving at Paris, he found Mrs. Butler in an extremely critical condition. She had been ill since the day following her arrival, and Dolores had scarcely slept or tasted food in her care and anxiety.

"Never since my uncle died," she said to Percy, "have I known such loneliness and dependence as I feel now. It seemed to me I must have someone near me, who would share my anxiety and personal interest in the patient. I hope you will forgive me for sending for you: but when I realized that she might die, I could not bear the suspense any longer alone."

Percy proved himself a hero in the emergency: he was brother, father, friend and messenger, all in one.

He performed all those innumerable outside duties necessitated by illness, and helped sustain Dolores' courage and strength, until at length the patient was pronounced on the highway to recovery.

Then there were long health-restoring drives, and pleasant afternoons when Percy read to the convalescent, while Dolores sat near with her sewing or drawing. But by and by there came a day when Percy realized that he must tear himself away, at once.

He had been reading aloud, and, among other things, he read a little poem entitled "The Farewell." It seemed particularly suited to his case.

'Tis not the untried soldier new to danger Who fears to enter into active strife. Amidst the roll of drums, the cannons' rattle, He craves adventure, and thinks not of life.

But the scarred veteran knows the price of glory, He does not court the conflict or the fray. He has no longing to rehearse that gory And most dramatic act, of war's dark play.

He who to love, has always been a stranger, All unafraid may linger in your spell. My heart has known the warfare, and its danger. It craves no repetition, so farewell.

He laid down the book. Mrs. Butler was asleep, lulled by his soothing voice. As he sat looking at Dolores, her beauty, her grace, her intellect, and all her countless charms awoke an irritated sense of injury in his heart.

What right had she to keep her attractions constantly before him, and yet deny him the right of possession? It was the cup of Tantalus. He rose suddenly.

"Dolores," he said, drawing a letter from his pocket, "I wrote this to you before I received your telegram calling me to you. I am going back to London day after to-morrow. I shall call to-morrow to say farewell. But I want you to read this letter, as it will explain to you my abrupt leave-taking better than I can explain it." And then he left her.

Dolores broke the seal, and began to read the letter, first with wondering curiosity, then with anger. Her eye flashed, her cheek flushed, her lip quivered.

"What right has he to address me, to think of me like this?" she cried bitterly. "I have never given him one liberty" Then she paused, for over her swept the memory of that single moment on the ice-boat when her heart had rested against his, her head pillowed upon his shoulder. Even now, it thrilled her with an emotion as sweet as it was strange. Her anger gave place to a profound melancholy.

Dimly, and with a sensation approaching terror, she began to understand Percy's own feelings, and the danger of his position. She could not blame him, she could only blame herself.

"It is my own fault," she said to her aching heart. "I expected too much. There is no possibility of an enduring friendship between man and woman in this world. That, too, is as transient and unreliable as love. And yet, and yet, how can I give up my friend, how can I?" and, burying her face in her hands, she sobbed aloud.

When Percy called the following day, Mrs. Butler was informed, for the first time, of his intended return to America the succeeding week.

"Then we must be ready to accompany you," she said. "I am convinced that I have only a short time to live. I want to die in my own land. Dolores, we can be ready, can we not, by the time Percy goes?"

"It is not necessary," Dolores replied, blushing painfully. "We could go the next week as well. We need not trouble Mr. Durand to act as our escort on this voyage, Mrs. Butler."

"Why, what in the world has come over you?" cried Mrs. Butler, staring with wondering eyes at Dolores. "You speak as if Percy were a stranger, instead of our almost brother and son. I am sure he will wait for us, if we cannot go next week. I have an unaccountable dread of making the voyage unattended. I shall feel far safer with our friend by my side; and, somehow, I am sure we shall need him."

So again Percy's earnest desire to fly from an embarrassing position was circumvented, and he was once more to be the companion of Dolores.

Mrs. Butler seemed to rally with a feverish excitement as they made their preparations for departure. Dolores watched her with anxious eyes.

"I fear you are not strong enough to take the sea-voyage at this time of year," she urged. "Will you not wait until later in the season, dear Mrs. Butler?"

But Mrs. Butler would not listen. "I can scarcely wait until next week;" she said, "I could not possibly delay my departure another month. It would make me ill, I know. Once on the ocean I shall grow stronger."

But instead she drooped, and failed; and on the fifth day of the stormy voyage, Percy and Dolores stood beside her shrouded form listening to the solemn service for the dead at sea.

They were standing on the deck, quite alone, the evening before they reached harbor....

Dolores drew a long shivering sigh. "Oh," she said, "I dread the sight of land! It seems to me, I am going into some arid desert, where I shall faint, and die, from very loneliness. I have lost my friend who was almost like an own mother to me. And now I am to lose you. Life is cruel to me. I think it is wicked for parents to bring children into this world of trouble and sorrow. Oh, why was I ever born to swell the tide of miserable suffering humanity?"

Percy laid his hand gently on her arm.

"You do not lose my friendship," he said. "Remember, I shall always be your loyal friend, ready to do you any favor. But the close companionship and intimate association of the last year becomes every day more impossible. You must realize it yourself."

"I do, I do," she said, and then she put her hands over her face, and her tears fell through the slender fingers.

"I wish I had been buried in the sea, too;" she sobbed. "I would not have been so much alone as I am upon this dreary earth, where every thing dear is taken from me."

He turned and took her hands down from her tear wet face, and drew them closely in his own.

His face was very pale. His voice trembled with the intensity of his emotions.

"Listen to me Dolores," he said, in a low, and almost stern tone. "I think we understand and respect each other's views perfectly. I think, if in a moment of profound sorrow like this, we disregarded the settled convictions of a life-time, that we should in calmer and brighter hours regret it. But I think also, that when two people have become so necessary to each other's lives as we have become, when such perfect sympathy exists, as exists between us, I think then, Dolores, that it is wicked to throw aside the happiness which might be theirs. George Eliot and Mr. Lewes did not throw it away; Shelley and Mary Godwin did not; Mary Wollstonecraft and Imlay did not. It is simply a question whether a woman cares more for the forms of Society, and the laws made by men, than she cares for the love and companionship of one man. I have found more happiness in this year of association with you, than I supposed it possible for life to afford me. You are to me an ideal comrade: I can picture years of such companionship; happy wanderings, sweet home-comings, quiet evenings, cosy suppers, and all with the perfect knowledge that it might cease at any time either or both wearied of it; all with the knowledge that the individual liberty of each was absolutely untrammeled; and that, when love ceased to exist, there were no bonds to fetter. It seems to me that happiness, as perfect as it ever exists in this world, might bless such an union of two lives. Dolores, will you accept the love and protection I offer you?"

Her hands had rested passive in his, while she listened. Her face was turned from him, her eyes gazing out over the expanse of sea. Not a sail was in sight. One solitary gull flapped lonesome wings above the inhospitable waves. It seemed to her that her life was like that gull's, the world stretched before her, like a great waste of water, shoreless and desolate. She thought of the monotonous years awaiting her, homeless and alone as she was; of the ghastly emptiness of every pleasure, if she no more saw his face, no more heard his voice. She shivered slightly, and his hands tightened their clasp upon her own. His touch thrilled her with a sweet inexplicable joy. She ceased to reason or think.

Turning her white, beautiful, strangely calm face up to his, she answered solemnly and distinctly:

"I will."

And just then a star shot down from heaven, and sank into the dark and troubled waters of the sea below.

CHAPTER XIV. ONE MAN AND ONE WOMAN

Sitting in her bijou apartments, which consisted of a handsome "Flat" in a quiet and respectable portion of New York, Dolores seemed lost in pleasant reverie, when her little French maid, Lorette, appeared before her.

"Everything is done but the dusting of this room, Madame," she said, in her native tongue. "Will Madame sit in the boudoir now"

"No, Lorette, you can go," Dolores answered, speaking French with as fine an accent as the Parisian née. "I will finish dusting, and as I am to dine out with Monsieur to-day, you need not return before to-morrow."

Lorette, who came every morning to attend to the domestic duties of the little ménage, gladly took her congé, and Dolores flitted gayly about, dust-brush in hand, singing a merry snatch of opera, pausing at every sound, to listen for a familiar step, the perfect picture of a happy, expectant housewife making ready for the return of a loved one. Presently a quick footstep bounded up the stairs, and Dolores flew to the door before the latch-key could turn the lock, swung it wide open, and was closely clasped in the arms of Percy, who greeted her with a gay "Bon matin, chère amie! and how have you been all these days?" Then, noticing the dust-brush on the floor beside her: "Why! how is this? has Lorette failed to make her appearance, that my lady-love has to perform her duties?"

"Oh, no! I sent her away," smiled Dolores. "I knew we did not need her to-day and" (shyly) "I did not want any third person to mar our greeting after your long absence."

"Long!" Percy repeated, laughing, as he threw himself into an easy chair, and drew her down on an ottoman at his side. "Long? three days, ma petite? I am often absent from you as long as that."

"You have never before been absent from the city so long as that, in this year of our new life," she said, as she caressed his hands, "without taking me with you, mon ami."

"Well, but I often stay away from this charming nest, that length of time, without seeing you!"

"So long as I know you are in the city I am not lonely. The air I breathe seems impregnated with your breath, and I am happy and contented to await your coming. If I walk down street, I feel a kindly interest in the throngs of people I meet, because perchance you may be among them. But when you are out of town the whole world seems depopulated. Yesterday I walked on Broadway a little while, but the people all looked like ghastly phantoms to me. Because you were not, I knew, among them, there seemed to be no life, no beauty in the moving shapes. I hurried home and hid myself in these rooms, so full of memories of you."

Sweet as were her words of love and devotion, they cast a faint shadow on her listener's face.

"I am afraid you allow yourself to be too melancholy during my absence!" he said. "It makes me sad to think of you so lonely, I like to think of you as happy and contented always."

"Oh, I am, I am!" she hastened to reply. "How could I help being happy in this ideal life of ours? We are so independent of the world, so in harmony with our own principles, so true to each other, Oh, Percy! I do not think two people could be happier then we are; do you? Are you not perfectly happy with me, dear?"

Just for one second Percy hesitated before he replied. Then he met the anxious look of inquiry in Dolores' eyes, and answered:

"Yes, perfectly: or rather, I am happier in my companionship with you than I have been in many years. I know my life is better, too, in many ways, and my thoughts fairer, than in my old restless days of adventure. Yet, of course, no lot is without its annoyances and troubles. Did you ever think how strange it is, that man expects a whole eternity of unalloyed bliss, from a Ruler who denies him a single month of it here?"

Dolores shook her golden head.

"I used to speculate a great deal about the next world," she said. "I read all kinds of books on the subject, and I grew very much confused. Finally, I rested back on the orthodox ideas, as quite as sensible as any. I am sure the world and human nature is inclined to evil. I think it is a misfortune to exist, and that we need a future life to repay us for all we endure here. And I am sure it will require a Mediator to ever reconcile the Creator to us or to give us eternal joy; but we can attain it if we seek the way."

"I do not believe that we can attain any joys we have not earned here," Percy replied. "I do not believe in sudden conversions, or death-bed repentance, or being cleansed by blood. That faith gives a man too much latitude altogether. Every violated principle, every indulged appetite, every selfish or mean act or thought, I think will count against us on the last day, no matter how we repent at death's door, or how we cry out to be saved. Salvation depends upon ourselves, and the use we make of our time on earth. We are shaping our spirits by our daily lives while in the body. Just as we have shaped them, beautiful or hideous, they will appear before God when our bodies fall away and leave them bare. We cannot in a moment's space, expect any power to remove the scars we have made by a life-time of wrongdoing. It would not be a just power if it did. Why should the man who has lived in sin all his life be cleansed by crying to Christ on his death-bed, and permitted to enter into just such joys as the good man has earned by a life of noble deeds? I do not believe in a creed like that."

Dolores put a soft hand over his mouth.

"Let us not talk religion," she said. "I fear you are a sad heretic. Yet I agree with you that every violated principle counts against us. But we need not fear death on that account, Percy. I am living up to my highest convictions of right: are not you?"

Again Percy hesitated. Then he laid his hand on her golden head, and looked gravely in her sweet eyes, as he answered:

"Sometimes, Dolores, I do not feel that I am. Sometimes the fears that you may one day repent our independent course of action, together with the fact that we are obliged to hide so much of our companionship from the world, weighs upon me like a burden."

She caught his hand and held it against her cheek.

"It must not, it must not!" she cried. "I shall never repent these perfect days with you, never. We have violated no principles. All laws are made by man, and every nation has its own peculiar ideas and rules upon this subject. I believe God blesses and approves of our companionship. You tell me that your life is better for it, and I know I am ten-fold more unselfish, and womanly, and sympathetic than ever before. Surely, we have been a benefit and strength to each other. As for secrecy, I am ready, and willing to meet the world at any time, Percy, proudly, as George Eliot met it. I am not ashamed of my love for you, or my devotion to you. I have never asked for secrecy."

Percy flushed slightly.

"I know you have not," he answered. "But the world condemns, without trial, who ever dares defy its opinions. Were we to publicly declare our ideas, we should be subjected to a thousand annoyances which we escape now. Cranks and villains would make no distinction between our sweet comradeship and their own immoral lives, while Society would exile us wholly, and people in general would cry us down. For your sake, as well as for my own social and business interests, it seems wiser to keep our pleasant seclusion."

"Yet Society is full of disgraceful intrigue, the very best of it," cried Dolores, with scorn. "The very people who would condemn us for our ideas, are hiding shameful infidelities in their own lives."

"Some of them," Percy admitted, "not all. Many a man among my acquaintances, who would mark my name off his visiting list, if we were to make our beliefs public, is himself similarly situated, save that he is also deceiving a wife; while I wrong no third party. But in the eyes of men, you know, the sin consists in being found out."

"Thank heaven, I am not in the position of one of those deceived wives!" cried Dolores, fervently. "At the first moment you tire of me, or that your heart strays away from me, you are free to go, without hesitating, and without legal proceedings. I should not want you to remain after you ceased to love me. You know my maxim is, 'those who love are wed, and those who no longer love are no longer wed.'"

Dolores really believed what she said. It is so easy to be liberal and broad in our theories, before our weak, human hearts are put upon the rack.

Percy, who enjoyed the sensation of liberty which her words gave him, felt also moved by an affectionate admiration for the lovely speaker. He reached out his arms and drew her fair head against his heart.

"I shall never tire of you, my royal lady!" he said, kissing her brow and cheek. "You combine all the qualities necessary to keep me true. You are a bright mental companion, a beautiful picture to my eye, and a fond heart-friend. And then you never hamper my liberty, or fret me by asking where I have been, or whither I am going, or why I have not come home sooner, as so many wives do. I appreciate your delightful good sense, when I see how some of my friends are martyrs to the whims of exacting women."

"It seems to me," Dolores replied, "that a woman makes a great mistake, who expects a man to give up all his old friends, and pleasures, and devote every moment of his life to her: and to account to her for every hour passed out of her presence. It must be terribly galling to a man who has been accustomed to his liberty. I think men are like some spirited horses, the tighter you draw the rein, the more reckless their pace: while with an easy rein they jog along very sedately. But speaking of our happiness, dear, I read a little poem the other day in an old book, which reminded me of our love. May I read it to you?"

Percy looked at his watch:

"Yes, if it is not very long:" he said. "We must be off for our drive in half an hour."

Dolores ran and brought an old magazine from her ebony desk, and, resuming her place at Percy's knees, read the poem.

"The name of the author is not given," she said; "but it seemed to me whoever wrote it, had loved as we love, Percy, with every faculty of his being. It is called

THREE-FOLD.

Somewhere I've read a thoughtful mind's reflection: "All perfect things are three-fold:" and I know Our love has this rare symbol of perfection: The brain's response, the warm blood's rapturous glow, The soul's sweet language, silent and unspoken. All these unite us, with a deathless tie. For when our frail, clay tenement is broken, Our spirits will be lovers still, on high.

My dearest wish, you speak before I word it. You understand the workings of my heart. My soul's thought, breathed where only God has heard it, You fathom with your strange divining art. And like a fire, that cheers, and lights, and blesses, And floods a mansion full of happy heat, So does the subtle warmth of your caresses, Pervade me with a rapture, keen as sweet.

And so sometimes, as you and I together Exult in all dear love's three-fold delights, I cannot help but vaguely wonder whether When our freed souls, attain their spirit heights, E'en if we reach that upper realm where God is, And find the tales of heavenly glory true, I wonder if we shall not miss our bodies, And long, at times, for hours on earth we knew.

As now, we sometimes pray to leave our prison And soar beyond all physical demands, So may we not sigh, when we have arisen, For just one old-time touch of lips and hands? I know, dear heart, a thought like this seems daring Concerning God's vast Government above, Yet, even There, I shrink from wholly sparing One element, from this, our Three-fold Love."

"What a very queer idea!" commented Percy, with a slight frown, as Dolores finished reading the poem. "It has the merit of being original, at least, but I cannot say that I like it."

"Still it expresses a great deal: the person who composed it must have comprehended every phase of love. Do you not think so?"

"It is quite as likely that the author had never loved at all, save in imagination. And I do not like the idea of ever longing for my body after I once get through with its troublesome demands. It is too material."

Dolores looked wonderingly at Percy.

"What a strange man you are!" she said. "After all, I do not think I fully understand you. Sometimes you shock me with your lack of orthodoxy, and again I feel as if your spiritual nature was far beyond my own in its development. You are a paradox, mon ami. But there is the carriage, and I must put on my hat and gloves."

CHAPTER XV. SUDDEN FLIGHT

As Percy ran down the stairs to the street door one day, his mind was in a very contented state.

This unfettered life with a thoroughly congenial companion, who lived wholly for him, and yet laid not one restriction upon his liberty, what could be more delightful?

He had all the comforts and benefits of a home, with none of the care or monotony of domestic life.

"I am the most fortunate of men," he mused, as he stopped on the lower landing to light his cigar. "Among the thousands in this city who have their agreeable companions hidden away like choice gems from the eyes of the world, I doubt if there is another Dolores. So beautiful, so true, so sensible, and so perfectly satisfied with her situation. Surely I am an ungrateful dog to ever feel discontented and restless, as I do so often."

He opened the street door, and came face to face with Homer Orton.

They greeted each other cordially, and passed down the street together.

One of the first remarks the journalist made, put to flight all Percy's sense of happy security and seclusion, and rendered him miserable during the entire day.

"By the way," Homer said, "do you know if Miss King, at whose rooms we met in Paris, is in New York? I was almost positive I saw her on Broadway, recently."

Percy's heart fairly chilled with fear. Not for the world would he have Homer Orton know, that Dolores was living in the very block from which he had just emerged. For her sake, for both their sakes, this must not be.

"It does not seem possible, that it could have been Miss King:" he answered, evasively. "I gave her my address in Europe, and she promised faithfully to inform me at once, if she returned to America at any time, even for a brief visit."

"Well, I might have been mistaken," Homer continued, unsuspectingly. "But it certainly was a striking resemblance. What a beautiful creature she was! Too bad she was so carried away with her hobbies, though. I used to think you might be able to talk her out of them, if any one could, and overcome her objections to marriage."

"I am not a marrying man," Percy answered, coldly, "and I respected the lady's views too much to wish her to change them. Good morning."

He felt annoyed and irritated all day, at the recollection of his morning encounter with Homer Orton.

But his annoyance settled into absolute alarm, when, two days later, he met the journalist again, precisely at the same place.

"Are your rooms in this block?" asked Homer, in some surprise, as he greeted his friend. "If so, we are near neighbors. I am boarding in the block above."

"No I have been calling on a friend," Percy answered, boldly. "He is ill, and I drop in often to see him." And then he hastened to change the conversation.

He pondered on the situation all that day. Something evidently must be done. With the journalist so near, Dolores was liable to be seen by him any day, and then, who could say, that the story might not appear with large headlines in the morning papers. It would make an excellent sensation article. But even if the journalist should not make it public, the very fact that he knew of Dolores' presence in America would destroy all their comfort.

Before night, he resolved upon an expedient. Recently he had been making some investments in South America. He had intended to visit Valparaiso to look after his affairs, sometime in the future. Why not go at once, and take Dolores with him? She was the most charming of traveling companions, and the journey, which might occupy two or three months, if they chose to make it, would be one more delightful experience to add to their many adventures.

And the journalist would no doubt have changed his location ere their return. Newspaper men never remained long in one place, he knew.

Before another week had elapsed the two comrades set forth upon their journey.

It was nearly sunset. Two Americans, with native guides, who had been leisurely making the wonderful trip from Arequipa to Santiago, in Spanish saddles, were approaching a canyon, nine thousand feet above the sea level. All day their gentle mules had carefully picked their way on mere shelves of rock, twisting back and forth through fissures and crevices that presented a kaleidoscopic scene to their wondering eyes.

Suddenly emerging from the narrow mountain pass, a valley burst upon their view, like some beautifully-set stage scene when the curtain rises. The area of the valley was not more than three acres: but all around it were the giant steeples of Andean granite rising in tapering lines to the very clouds: every crevice, every seam, covered with a magnificent verdure of trailing vines, hundreds of feet in length, and heavy with delicate-leaved blossoms. At the base of these mountains the cactus grows to perfection; such gorgeousness of bloom bewilders the credulity of travelers. Ferns that are indescribable in their sensitiveness of texture, interlaced this marvelous floral display: and from various directions out from the fissured rocks, flashed and sparkled bright rivulets, as they leaped from point to point until lost in some underground cavern.

The guides swung the hammocks; the mules were unloaded and allowed the freedom of the plateau. Off under a young palm the kettles were swinging, while supper was prepared for the tired and hungry travelers.

As they arose from their repast of boiled yam, fried plantain, smoked fish, and cocoa milk, with dessert of mangoes and pines, Dolores noticed the guides busily setting fire to a quantity of shrubs they had gathered during the day. This shrub was heavily charged with capsicum qualities, and at once filled the air with a stifling cayenne odor.

"What in the world are those men doing?" asked Dolores, with her handkerchief to her mouth. "Do you suppose they are observing some religious rite?"

Percy laughed as he assisted Dolores into her hammock, and swung himself into his own close beside her.

"I fancy the ceremony you see will be of more practical benefit to us, than any religious rite;" he said. "The guides are burning the potéké, a native shrub, which brings sure deliverance from insects; lizards, gnats, bugs and reptiles of all descriptions take an unceremonious departure when that peppery perfume fills the air. We shall be insured of a good night's rest by that means."

"Yes, if we are not choked to death by the odor," Dolores mumbled from the folds of her handkerchief.

"Oh, Percy, look!"

Percy looked in the direction indicated by Dolores, and his eyes were greeted by a phenomenon seen only in the plateaus of the Andes. It was the duplicating lines of the departing sun, upon the castellated rocks, as they pierced between the apexes and the basin. They reached in like silver threads, then flushed to gold and amber, as they fell deeper and deeper into the valley and rested in a trinity of colors upon the wonderful foliage, or hung like rainbows above the glittering brooks.

Percy and Dolores gazed, silent and almost breathless, while the long lines of glory changed to softest amethyst and gray. The guides were sleeping soundly; the tired mules were knee-deep in wild clover; in among the leaves of the india-rubber trees, a bright-plumaged arajojo sang out his saucy Ta-ha-ha, Ta-ha-ha.

Dolores reached out her hand and clasped Percy's, in the fading glory of the wonderful sunset.

"Oh, love!" she sighed, "I wish God would let us die to-night, life is so perfect. And something tells me we are never to be so happy on earth again."

CHAPTER XVI. A MAN AND TWO WOMEN

Soon after their return, Percy was called to Centerville, a large village a few hours' ride from New York. He had established a Mr. Griffith there in business, some months previous to his South American trip, and now their affairs needed overhauling and examining.

Being detained over Sunday, Percy strolled out for a walk after his late breakfast. Centerville was not well provided with schools or other public buildings; but like the majority of large villages, it boasted several imposing church edifices.

The day was warm, and crowned with an Indian summer haze. As he strolled by a costly stone temple of worship, out through the open windows floated a voice so pure, so beautiful, so magnetic, that he paused involuntarily to listen. It was a woman's voice, singing the old familiar hymn, but it held a new meaning for him as he listened:

"Guide me, oh, thou Great Jehovah, Pilgrim through a barren land! I am weak, but thou art mighty, Lead me with thy powerful hand."

Never in his life had Percy so realized his own finiteness, never had he so reverenced the Supreme Majesty of the Creator, as while he listened to that voice, singing the familiar words with indescribable pathos and passion.

Percy's fearless criticisms of creeds and dogmas had won for him, among people of illiberal thought, the undeserved reputation of an atheist.

The world is full of good-hearted, but short-sighted people, who brand any man as an infidel or lunatic, whose ideas of divine worship differ from their own.

Percy's whole nature was deeply reverential; but his conceptions of religion were too high and broad for the ordinary mind, accustomed to the well-worn ruts of thought to understand or even grasp. In his early boyhood, he had believed in every thing; church, woman, home, happiness. But one woman had wrecked him in mid-ocean; and he had thrown overboard all his old faiths in things human and divine, barely saving his life and reason.

Then, as time passed on, and his hurts healed, his inborn reverence for Something over and beyond himself returned. His belief in a future life was as fixed and firm as it was vague and undefined. But oftentimes he felt conscious of the near presence of his mother, the mother who had died when he was a youth and most needed her. And he knew that she lived, and loved him, and watched over him. It was her occasional presence, which convinced him, beyond the possibility of doubt, that death was only the gateway to a new life.

Always, when he was untrue to himself or his principles, her spirit fled away from him, and again she came so near, he could almost hear the rustle of her wings.

It was long months now, since she had come to him. Never in his dreams, never in his waking hours; and the sense of loneliness and longing was sometimes overwhelming.

But now, while he listened to that unseen singer's voice, his mother came back to him; there, in the golden haze of that Indian-summer morning, he felt as conscious of her near presence as if his eyes beheld her.

"Bread of heaven, Bread of heaven, Feed me till I want no more,"

sang the voice, and it seemed to ring up to the very courts of heaven with a great cry of hunger and longing.

Never had Percy so felt the craving in his own soul for heavenly manna, and for something beyond and greater than himself on which to lean, as at this moment.

It seemed to him, that he could not rest until he had looked upon the face of the singer.

He entered the church, and sat down in an unoccupied pew near the door.

The singing had ceased, and from his position the choir was entirely hidden from view by a curtain.

Percy sat through the long and tedious sermon, and listened with impatience to the dreary, uncomforting discourse.

"No wonder," thought he, "that the singer put so much pleading into her cry for 'Bread of heaven,' if she derives her spiritual sustenance from the droppings of this sanctuary. The weary soul would faint by the wayside, who depended upon such food."

The sermon seemed interminable, but it ended at last, to the gratification of the tired congregation. Again Percy heard that voice of heavenly beauty, soaring up to the very Throne in song; but, strive as he might, he could catch no glimpse of the singer.

He left the church, soothed, uplifted, but disappointed.

As he sat in his room at the hotel, late in the afternoon, writing letters, Mr. Griffith called.

"I saw you at church this morning," he said, "and my wife sent me around to bring you home to tea. She thought it might be dull for you here at the hotel, and though we are plain folks, we shall be glad to have you come and take common fare with us."

"You are very kind," Percy answered, "but I ought to finish these letters"

"Never mind the letters," insisted Mr. Griffith. "My wife will feel hurt if you don't come; and we can promise you some good music, at least. Maybe you noticed our soprano singer in the choir this morning. She boards with us, and we think she's about as good as any of your city singers. There is no service to-night at the church, and when there is not, she always sings for us at home. People fairly hang on the gates to listen. I hope you'll come."

"Thank you!" said Percy, with alacrity, rising and pushing aside his writing materials. "I will."

When he stood face to face with Helena Maxon, for it was our old friend, whom we greet again after more than five years. Percy felt a slight disappointment. It had seemed to him, that such a voice must belong to a creature as fair as the morning, an ethereal being, all gold and blue and white, like Aurora herself.

Instead, he saw a shapely form, inclined to be voluptuous in its curves, and a face absolutely without tints; a dusky head, and sombre eyes, and a skin like the brown side of a peach, and perfectly devoid of color, save in the full red lips of the rather large mouth.

"Her face is too round for beauty," he said, in his swift mental analysis, "and her mouth and nose are not classic. But what exquisite care she bestows upon her person; what perfectly-kept hands and teeth and hair! She radiates purity and cleanliness like a water-lily. And where did she learn her matchless charm and manner?"

As the conversation progressed, Percy's wonder grew. Miss Maxon's ready flow of words, her simple dignity and her animation, rendered her positively charming. He soon forgot her absence of tints; for as she talked, the light of her spirit seemed to shine through and brighten her face like sunlight shining through an autumn leaf. And the strange peculiarity of her eyes presently attracted him, and fascinated him with their mesmeric spell. So soon as Helena became interested in any subject on which she conversed, or in her music, or in the personality of her listeners, a delicate film, which had almost the appearance of smoke seen rising over the face of the heavens at night, completely enveloped her dark eyes. It seemed to shut out all material objects from her vision as if her soul drew a curtain before her sight, that it might better contemplate the wonders visible only to spiritual eyes. Yet through this curtain you felt conscious that her soul looked into yours.

It is a peculiarity seen only in the eyes of those possessed of clairvoyant powers; and it riveted Percy's gaze upon Helena's face, and fascinated him as no mere physical beauty had ever fascinated him.

By and by she sang, and again Percy felt himself lifted up into a new, rarified atmosphere, while he listened.

It was as if his soul projected itself out of his body, and floated up on the waves of her voice close to the spirit world.

Percy never knew quite how the conversation began: but after she had resumed her seat, he suddenly found himself telling her how peculiarly her singing had affected him.

"No doubt you will think me a sort of a lunatic!" he said. "But while you sang this morning, it seemed to me that my mother, who has been dead since my early manhood, came near to me. The impression lasted throughout the day: and it has brought me an inexpressible happiness."

A sudden light transfigured Helena's face, rendering it absolutely beautiful. She leaned slightly forward, with her hands clasped before her.

"Then you are susceptible to these impressions?" she said. "I am always pleased and interested in meeting any one who is. There are so few people in the world who realize how thin the veil is which divides us from our dear ones. Why, Mr. Durand, often when I am singing, I not only feel, I know that my father and my mother are close beside me, enveloping me with their love and sympathy. And then I sing, as I never sing at other times. The exhilaration of their presence fills me with a strength and ecstacy that is indescribable. I feel almost more than human."

She ceased speaking suddenly, and her face was luminous with a divine light. A subtle warmth and fragrance seemed to emanate from her; Percy felt thrilled and magnetized, with an influence as mysterious as it was powerful.

"Then your parents are not living?" he said, gently.

"Not here," she answered, with a sad smile. "They died in one year. My father was the victim of a violent fever which devastated our town: my mother grieved herself into the grave a few months later. It had been a perfect union; they were mental comrades, spiritual affinities, physical mates. They could not exist apart. It was better that she joined him so soon."

"It left you very much alone?" Percy spoke softly, scarcely knowing what to say in presence of such a bereavement.

"Yes, and no," she answered. "If I had believed they were lying in the earth waiting the Judgment Day, scores, thousands or millions of years hence, I should have been crazed with my desolation. But my faith was so comforting to me, however unorthodox, that I have found strength and happiness in it."

"Tell me what it is?" urged Percy, earnestly, almost eagerly. "These subjects interest and fascinate me. Long ago, my intellect rejected old dogmas. Yet I find it difficult to know what to believe. The worn out creeds insult my intelligence. The liberal teachers of the day shock me with their irreverence, and leave my soul hungry: and in Spiritualism I find so much trickery, fraud, and immorality, mixed up with a few mysterious and unsatisfactory truths, that I am again in despair."

"But you must not be in despair," Helena said, with one of her beautiful smiles. "You have not looked at Spiritualism from the right standpoint. So long as you seek its truths through professional mediums, you will be dissatisfied and confused."

"Then you think they are all humbugs?"

"Certainly not:" Helena replied, with emphasis. "There are people endowed with the gift of divination, beyond doubt. There are peculiarly organized beings who can read the future and the past, beings who see through and beyond this thin veil of mortality, into the spiritual realms which lie very close to us. But we must not look to those people for our enlightenment upon this subject. If we do, we soon lose our individuality; we grow dependent and unpractical and visionary. God placed us here to carve out our own destinies, to work and wait for events, not to tear aside the curtain and read the cypher which is understood by a few."

"But how, then, can I obtain the benefits you mention from this belief?" questioned Percy.

"You must look to the development of your own spiritual nature, and to the consequent crucifying of your baser self, in order to obtain the comfort and benefit of this belief. In this you will have the help of your departed friends."

"You think they retain their interest in and love for us, the same there as here?"

"Oh, yes, assuredly. Yet often our sorrows seem, to their enlarged vision, as the sorrows of children over broken toys seem to us; yet they strive to comfort us."

"If that is true," interposed Percy, "why was it, that after my mother died, and I used to lie awake at night, and plead with Heaven to let me feel her touch, or see her face, if only for a second, why did she not come to me?"

"Because," Helena answered gently, "there are restrictions upon their liberty, there are limits to their powers, even as there are to our own. They live higher, freer, more exalted lives, but they are not gods. I remember when I was first sent from home to boarding-school, how bitter was my homesickness and sorrow. I used to write tear-blotted letters to my mother, begging her to come to me. She did not come; other and more important duties detained her at home. She knew it was better for me to remain and overcome my loneliness. So your mother in the spirit world may have been detained by the wonderful tasks given her to do. Yet on other occasions she no doubt comes to you, as she came this morning. I think we cannot expect frequent companionship from these pure spirits, however, unless we cultivate the better part of our natures. They will not linger near us if we are wholly earthly in our aims and ambitions, and immoral in our lives."

"I believe that, I am certain of it in my own experience," Percy said, in a low voice. "Whenever I violate a principle, my mother flies from me as in fear. She has been absent many months, Miss Maxon, until your voice wooed her back."

"Therein lies the great religious lesson in this belief;" continued Helena. "I find that even my petty tempers, my uncharitable feelings, or thoughtless criticisms of other people, frighten away this holy company. I have to set a constant watch upon my mind and heart, to let no evil or selfish thought enter, if I would retain their helpful and loving influences. It is no easy task, Mr. Durand. It is constant warfare, between the material and the spiritual nature. But the results are glorious. Often when I have put to rout evil feelings, and selfish thoughts, back to my soul, like a flock of white doves, the spirits of comforting friends fly, lifting me into an atmosphere so heavenly and beautiful, that I seem scarcely to belong to earth. Oh surely, God could not give better employment to his angels, than to let them sometimes comfort us, like this. Surely, there is nothing irreverent or wrong in this belief."

"No, it is the sweetest of all beliefs," Percy answered. "It robs death of all its horrors, and it is a belief which is gaining ground. Do you not think so?"

"Yes, indeed, with the more intellectual classes. There was a time, when it was considered an evidence of ignorance to profess any faith in spirit aid. Now it is considered an evidence of ignorance to declare positively that there is nothing in it. But sensible believers do not waste their time in seeking after crude miracles, miracles which can help no human soul, and only serve to confuse and puzzle the intellect. They turn their attention rather to the development of their own higher natures, which enables them to understand and enjoy these beautiful truths."

"Do you believe that the spirits of our dear ones ever reveal themselves to us?" asked Percy, growing more and more interested. "Have you ever been blessed by such a vision?"

"Never, though I have longed for it. Yet I believe others have been so blessed. You know the Bible overflows with such occurrences. We have, there, the inspired record of the re-appearance upon earth after death, of Samuel, Moses, Elijah, and Christ himself. If we believe the Bible, we must believe these things occurred. And I think God loves his people now as dearly as He loved them then. But I have no belief in, and no patience with, the miserable artifice and wicked pretense of the so-called materializing mediums. I do not believe the lovely spirit of my dear mother could be shown to me through any cabinet, like a jack-in-a-box. The idea that the spirits of the intellectual dead have nothing better to do than move furniture or rap on ceilings and floors, is disgusting and nonsensical in my view. I am a good deal of a Swedenborgian: I think with him, that the body, the eye, is merely a telescope, through which the soul gazes. What the soul sees, and how far it sees, depends upon many conditions, just as a clear or a murky atmosphere, and the mechanism of his instrument, influences the observations of the astronomer. When the soul, and the body, and the spiritual atmosphere are all in perfect condition, I believe we can see the spirit forms about us. You know St. Paul says: 'Run your race in patience, for you are surrounded by a cloud of witnesses.' But in our gross material lives, these conditions seldom occur. As for myself, I am satisfied with the comfort and strength I receive through unseen presences. I do not ask, or seek anything more."

A spiteful-voiced clock on the mantel counted off eleven strokes.

Percy arose in sudden confusion.

"How inexcusably late I have remained," he said, "how can I ever obtain pardon"

"No excuse is necessary!" interposed Mrs. Griffith. "We all thank you for causing Miss Maxon to talk so freely. It is seldom she does, and we love to hear her conversation as well as her singing. Be sure and come again, Mr. Durand."

As he walked back to his hotel, in upon his strangely enlarged and enlightened vision, a sudden thought of Dolores darted. He stopped in the street and put his hand to his brow. "My God!" he cried, "how can I go back to her?"

CHAPTER XVII. A MAN, A WOMAN, AND SPIRITS

He did not go near her for three days. During all that time he was battling with his own soul.

So strange and powerful was the impression made by the conversation of Helena, that the whole current of his life seemed changed.

All his former independent course of action, which he had justified with a thousand arguments, all his selfish years of pleasure, all his Arcadian existence with Dolores, loomed up before him now as lawless and wicked.

"No wonder my mother's pure spirit fled from me to the most distant borders of the spirit world," he said. "How unworthy her sweet companionship I am and yet I might become worthy."

But how could he go to Dolores, and tell her that their life together was a terrible mistake: that they must part at once, and forever?

And if he did not, how could he ever hope to attain that ideal of high, noble manhood, which would alone fit him for the companionship of his mother's spirit, here or hereafter?

He suffered the agonies of the damned, all those days. He shunned the streets for fear of meeting Dolores: the Club seemed hateful to him, and he remained shut in his own apartments, a prey to gloomy thoughts.

And then one of those curious caprices of Fate occurred, which again compelled him to stifle the voice of his conscience.

It often seems in this life, when a soul is floundering in a net-work of Sin's weaving, striving to extricate itself, that the Devil, like a great spider, comes along and spins new meshes about it.

A messenger brought Percy a note from Dolores one day. He opened it hastily and read:

"MY DARLING:

"I am ill: threatened with a fever. No one but Lorette is with me. I am longing for you, and I am alarmed about you. You never remained so long away from me before, without sending me some message. The thought that you may be ill, and that I am not near you to minister to your needs, is maddening. Write to me, dear, and if you can, come to your sick and lonely

"DOLORES."

He was by her side within an hour. She reached out her arms, and pillowed her flushed face on his breast, weeping softly.

"Oh, Love!" she murmured. "I have felt so lonely, so deserted these last days. I think I have realized just what life would be without you: it would be an agony of desolation. I could not live."

Percy's heart writhed within him, as he stroked the beautiful head and soothed her with kind words. How could he ever stab that loving heart by telling her the change that had come over him, a change as thorough as it was sudden; a change that was the dawn of a possible new life for him.

"I cannot. It is too late; it would be more cruel than murder," he said to himself, and he drew Dolores into his arms, and comforted her as he would have comforted a sick child. She asked no explanation of his absence, and he made none.

Within a week he had carried her away to a quiet country resort, where she soon regained her health. But during her illness, there came to her, through the clairvoyant power of a loving heart, the knowledge that some mysterious change had taken place in Percy. He was kind, oh, very kind; so careful of her bodily comfort, so solicitous for her welfare.

And yet what was it?

"Is anything troubling you?" she asked him one day. "You do not seem like yourself."

"There are some business matters which annoy me," he said, evading her eyes. "My South American ventures are a failure, that is all, my dear, save a miserable lassitude and sideache, which Dr. Sydney says is due to a touch of malaria."

But she knew better.

They returned to New York, and then Percy was guilty of an act of rash folly, for a man who desired to escape a complication of troubles.

He sent Dolores a message, saying he was called out of town suddenly. Then he took the train for Centerville. It was Saturday afternoon, and he told himself, that he would merely attend divine service in the morning, listen to Helena's voice once more, and come away without being seen by any one.

But in his heart, he knew that this was impossible. And when Mrs. Griffith approached him after service, and urged him to accompany them home, and dine with them, he went, without offering one objection.

Helena greeted him with simple cordiality, and entertained him with the easy grace so natural to her. He was at peace with himself, in her presence, for the first time since he last saw her.

"How strange it is!" he mused, "I have seen the most beautiful women in the world, I have listened to the most famous singers; and yet, I am moved by the presence and voice of a simple village maiden as I have never been moved in my life before."

A sudden impulse came over him to tell her his story, to ask her advice, as they sat alone in the afternoon. Then he hesitated: what if she turned from him, shocked, angry, horrified? so he only said:

"I wish you would call some of your wise spirits, Miss Helena, and ask them to read me my future. I am in trouble, a trouble out of which I can see no pathway. I wish good angels would tell me how it is to end."

"But that is not the province of spirits," Helena answered. "People often make the great mistake of supposing that the departed know all that is to happen to us while we remain upon earth. The fact is, they know very little about it, and are too busily employed to give their time to finding out the future for us."

"But if their lives are so exalted and their vision so broad, I see no reason why they should not know."

"You will see when you come to think of it sensibly," Helena continued, with a smile. "Their lives are, compared to our own just as much broader, more useful and more important, as the lives of great thinkers and philosophers and reformers, are greater than the lives of little children. Shakespeare, Carlyle, Lincoln, George Eliot, all were wonderful people who grasped almost the whole of the universe with their minds. Yet not one of them, were they all alive to-day, could foretell the future life of Mrs. Griffith's little child, yonder. Not one could say what was to occur to him in the next ten years. They could help him by their example, and strengthen him by their philosophy, but no more, great as they were. Well, now, the spirits of the dead regard us as children at school. They are far beyond us, in knowledge and usefulness; they are ever ready to strengthen and encourage us, but they cannot predict events for us. There are some, no doubt, who were gifted with clairvoyance here, who keep the power there. But such spirits are often too busy to come at our call. And they know, too, that it is better for us to depend upon ourselves in a great measure. It is through self-dependence that we develope our individuality, and become fitted for the labors of this world and the next."

"Then you think the future life is one of labor?" Percy asked.

"It is one of usefulness and progression, certainly, or it is not worth living," she answered. "Who would want to live at all, if we never advanced in any way? And the beauty of that new life is, that every particle of progress we have made here, even if it has brought us no reward, will enable us to take an advanced place there. So soon as we are out of the body, we shall realize this in all its satisfying truth. Every hard struggle on earth, every conquered temptation, every sorrow, every trial endured, every labor well performed, we shall see has its splendid reward in fitting us for the most exalted position in that new life. Every particle of love and affection we have bestowed on objects which seemed to make a poor return or no return here, will be given to us in ten-fold strength and sweetness there. The more we love humanity, the more we shall be loved and the wider will be our capabilities of wonderful labors in the spirit world. The two most God-like emotions given to mortals to experience, are love and sympathy. If we give our love with prodigality, and sympathize with every human being who crosses our pathway in life, it really matters very little whether we are loved in return, or whether the world thanks us for our sympathy, or not. It is the act of loving and sympathizing which shapes the soul. And when the body falls away, the spirit that has given its affections and sympathies freely on earth will stand forth, a mighty and beautiful Power in the New Life, no matter what its creed or belief in the earth life has been."

Percy drew a long deep breath. Again the delicate curtain was drawn over her dark eyes, softening and half concealing their sombre splendor. Again he felt that subtle warmth and fragrance emanating from her person, and was thrilled and magnetized by it.

"It is no earthly odor," he said. "It is the perfume of her soul."

"How clear and beautiful you make it all seem!" he said, aloud. "To listen to your words makes one long for death. And yet, if our lives have been selfish, immoral, unworthy, if we have wasted our time in mere earthly or sensual pleasures, how terrible must be the consciousness of it to the freed spirit."

"Yes, terrible, indeed. There comes the real hell of the suffering conscience. The soul will see its fearful mistake, and see how long and dreary is the pathway before it. Yet, it will realize, that God has left that lonely path open for it, and that it may by hard toil climb up to the position it might have occupied at the hour of its entering on the new life. I think the capability of a soul to suffer at that time, must be beyond our comprehension. It is terrible on earth to realize our lost opportunities. It will be far more intense there. But even the most depraved will be given a chance to rise, through centuries of striving. There is no eternal damnation, any more than there is instantaneous salvation."

Percy rose to go, stirred to the very depths of his better nature by her words. As he made his adieus, he said:

"Miss Maxon, will you write to me? I am in great trouble, as I told you; a trouble that seems to shut out every particle of light from the universe. Your words afford me the only comfort I have had for weeks. Will you write to me and cheer me a little through the gloomy days that lie before me?"

Helena's heart welled full of sympathy toward all the suffering world. Her creed of life was, to give all the comfort, and help, and cheer, possible to every troubled mortal on life's highway. She was never afraid to reach out her hand to a weak fallen creature, for fear of soiling it.

It is the woman, who feels herself the strongest and most secure in her virtue and her social position, who is most fearless in her efforts to uplift the unfortunate: and a very benevolent heart, is seldom coupled with a cautious brain.

There was such real suffering in Percy's face and voice, that Helena's heart was moved with pity. She held out her hand and looked him full in the eyes, her own full of sweetest sympathy.

"Yes, I will write to you," she said. "I am very sorry for you, if you are in such trouble. But you must remember, that in this life, to grow means to suffer. I found actual happiness in pain, when I fully realized the truth of that."

"But you have never suffered, and made another suffer, by your own selfish folly," Percy said, as he turned away. "Good by, and God bless you for your promise to write to me."

CHAPTER XVIII. APPLES OF SODOM

He went away a thousand times more hopelessly entangled in the meshes of fate than ever.

He loved Helena with a passion that frightened him, so mysterious, so sudden, so exalted, so intense in its spiritual force was it.

He who said that love, to be sincere, must be of slow growth, that man was a fool.

As God said, unto the darkened world, "Let there be light" and there was light, so, unto many a slumbering heart, He has said, "Let there be love," and there was love, radiant, glorious, eternal, as is the splendor of the sun in the heavens.

So had love sprung to life in the heart of Percy Durand, a love that the waters of death could not quench.

"Never since my mother died," he whispered to his heart, "have I felt such an adoring affection bordering upon worship, as I feel for this girl. I could be anything, do anything, with her beside me; my guide, my friend, my mate, my wife."

Wife! Yes, that was how he thought of Helena. All his old theories and cynical beliefs fell away from him, like dead leaves from a tree, in the presence of this beautiful new love.

All his old life of license, and bachelor freedom, and secret companionship with a charming woman, seemed like the apples of Sodom to him now.

He wanted a home where he could proudly welcome the whole world, if need be, to witness his happiness. He wanted a wife to entertain his friends, not a mistress to hide from them; and he wanted children to crown his life and perpetuate his name.

These highest human instincts come knocking at the door of every man's heart, some time in his life.

He may bolt the door with avarice or pride, curtain the windows with lawless passions, and block the entrance with worldly ambitions and pleasure. But the Creator who meant him to be a part of that holy earthly trinity, father, mother, and child, shall send a great unrest upon his soul; and despite all his precautions, a longing for the love of a pure woman and a little child shall take possession of his heart.

That time had come to Percy: come as suddenly and unexpectedly as the greatest eras almost always come in human existence.

He closed his eyes and indulged in wild dreams.

He saw himself sitting before an open fire-place: a little distance from him, Helena, in flowing white robes, singing a golden-haired child to sleep upon her breast. Near by, a friend, some of his bachelor companions, perhaps, envying his happiness, as he looked upon the scene with admiring eyes.

Then he sprang up and fairly groaned aloud.

"I must guard myself in my letters," he said. "I will only write to Helena, as a suffering man might address a Sister of Charity. She shall never know how I love her, until my life is free from every fetter of sin and folly, and until I have made myself worthy by years of noble living."

But you may as well talk of hiding the glory of the sunrise from the earth, as the fervor of a great passion from the object which inspired it.

Careful as were his expressions, his letters breathed an atmosphere of love as passionate as his mysterious sorrow seemed hopeless.

Helena's nature was deeply romantic and profoundly sympathetic. These letters, therefore, appealed to the strongest elements of her being.

All through her girlhood she had jealously guarded her heart's vast store of intense love for an ideal lover whom she had never yet seen.

And now through the medium of an earnest sympathy she was bestowing upon Percy all the lavish wealth of her rich nature, just as one might give a five-dollar gold piece, thinking it was only a shining penny, to a mendicant. She lived in a dream world; she performed her duties as music teacher and choir singer mechanically. The people with whom she associated were shadowy and unreal forms. The only person who really existed for her, was Percy, with his load of mysterious sorrow, which she and her glorious horde of spirit friends would somehow lift from him.

With her slight knowledge of the world at large, and society as it exists in cities, Helena had no comprehension of what that sorrow might be. She did not puzzle her head to divine it. She was willing to wait Percy's own time. Whatever it was, she knew he deserved her sympathy and her prayers.

Almost daily Percy saw Dolores. Each day he promised himself, that he would tell her what was in his heart. Each day he delayed the dreaded scene.

Upon Dolores, the terrible and overwhelming conviction was forcing itself, that Percy no longer loved her. The thought of a rival never once presented itself to her. She knew that she was beautiful, accomplished, congenial, everything, in fact, which he could desire in a companion.

"But," she reasoned, "it is a man's nature to tire of that which is his. Somewhere I have read, 'who ever gives too much in love, is certain not to receive enough in return;' and I am proving it true. It would be the same, were I his wife."

Then, in spite of herself, back upon her mind rushed the recollection of a quotation once made by Mrs. Butler in her arguments in favor of marriage: "If the fickle husband goes, he returns; but the lover, once gone, he never returns." She remembered how scornfully she had regarded such an argument. "What woman of pride or self-respect would desire the fickle husband to return?" she had said. "I should want him to go speedily, the moment his heart strayed from me, or tired of me. And better by far, for both, if there were no legal ties to sever."

All this sophistry she recalled now, with a dull pain at her heart. The time had come, when she felt positive, that Percy no longer loved her. Yet she could not tell him to go. The very thought of a separation was like a knife in her breast.

"How vain it is to assert what we would do in any situation in life," she said, "until we have loved. Love changes everything, even to one's whole nature. May God help me to bear this."

She had an instinctive knowledge, that Percy was trying to summon courage to tell her of his changed feelings. She shrank from it, as from a blow.

"I cannot hear him say the words," she moaned. "I cannot live and hear them from his lips; and I cannot let him go, I cannot, I cannot."

She grew thin and hollow-eyed, and the pathos of her face was heartrending. She tried to be cheerful and amuse Percy with her old flow of wit and anecdote. They took their usual drives, and indulged in theatres, and petits soupers afterward, as of old, but it was all a melancholy failure, a farce of their former happy days. Though he gave her the same gallant attentions, she knew his heart was not in it.

It was like looking on the dead face of a dear one: the features unchanged, but the spirit fled.

One day as he sat smoking a cigar in their pretty artistic rooms, while Dolores played a melancholy air on the piano, he determined to tell her of his resolution to leave her and go abroad. "I will not tell her that I love another," he thought; "that will give needless pain. But I cannot keep up this farce any longer. It must end."

"Dolores," he said, throwing away his cigar, "come and sit beside me on this ottoman. I want to talk with you."

She turned a pale, startled face to his, and her hands fell upon discordant keys.

"I will," she said, rising hurriedly, "in a moment. But first let me show you such a strange, sad little poem I found among some of Mrs. Butler's clippings to-day. Once I could not have understood such a sentiment. To-day I do. I remember showing you a poem that I thought applicable to ourselves another time, Percy. This is very unlike it."

She placed the slip of paper in his hand, and sat down beside him while he read it: her elbows resting on his knees, her brow bent on her clasped hands.

This was what he read:

When your love begins to wane, Spare me from the cruel pain Of all speech that tells me so. Spare me words, for I shall know.

By the half-averted eyes By the breast that no more sighs, By the rapture I shall miss From your strangely-altered kiss,

By the arms that still enfold But have lost their clinging hold, And, too willing, let me go, I shall know, love, I shall know.

Bitter will the knowledge be, Bitterer than death to me. Yet, 'twill come to me some day, For it is the sad world's way.

Make no vows, vows cannot bind Changing hearts or wayward mind. Men grow weary of a bliss Passionate and fond as this.

Love will wane. But I shall know, If you do not tell me so. Know it, tho' you smile and say That you love me more each day,

Know it by the inner sight That forever sees aright. Words could but increase my woe, And without them, I shall know.

When he had finished the reading, he turned and drew Dolores' white, suffering face against his breast without a word.

She lay there weeping silently, and neither spoke. But both hearts were full of unutterable pain and despair.

She clung to him as he rose to go.

"You will come to-morrow?" she said.

"Not to-morrow," he answered, gently. "I am going out of town for the day. But I will come again soon."

At the door he turned and looked back, his eyes full of infinite pity. Oh! how gladly he would have bestowed upon her the love that had so strangely gone out to Helena, had it been in his power.

"If God, among his gifts to mortals, had given us the ability to transfer an unwise love, how much misery we should be saved," he thought, as he went out.

CHAPTER XIX. A STORY AND A REVELATION.

Percy found himself so ill the next morning, that he was obliged to send for his physician, Dr. Sydney.

Ever since his return from South America, he had been losing strength and flesh, and a dull ache in his side, and darting pains throughout his entire body had rendered his nights restless, and his days full of lassitude. His physician had answered him that it was a "touch of malaria, contracted in the beastly climate of South America," and Percy had relied on quinine and time to effect a cure.

(We all know how customary it is in these days for physicians to designate any puzzling ailment by the convenient and indefinable term of malaria.)

But this morning, when Dr. Sydney was called to his patient, he decided that something more serious, and tangible than a touch of malaria was imminent.

Percy had been suffering from a hard chill during the night, which was now succeeded by a high fever, and acute pain in his side. He was sitting in his chair by the window, dressed as if to go out.

"My dear fellow, this will never do!" Dr. Sydney cried. "You are on the eve of a serious sickness, I fear, and you must be put to bed, and place yourself under treatment."

"Pshaw, nothing of the kind!" Percy answered. "I have taken cold, and beside, I am worn out with worry over some matters. That is all."

"H'm! then why did you send for me, if you know so much better about it than I do!" growled the old physician.

"Simply, because I want you to brace me up, and get me in condition to take a short trip on business this afternoon."

"A trip, business!" echoed Dr. Sydney, gazing at Percy over his spectacles. "Why, if you are not insane you will at once give up that idea. You will not be fit to leave your room under a week, if you do in that time: and you must have a good nurse, and keep perfectly quiet until you are out of this."

"But I tell you, I must attend to some important business out of town to-day!" Percy answered, stubbornly. "It is the worry and anxiety over the matter which has caused my illness, mainly. And I want you to give me a tonic, or a stimulant, or something that will carry me through the day. Then, if to-morrow I find myself no better, I will promise to go to bed and follow your advice. For I want to get in condition to go abroad very soon."

Finding his patient incorrigible, Dr. Sydney grimly prepared some medicine for him to take during the forenoon, and left him with a last injunction to be very careful of himself if he desired to escape a long siege of illness.

"But he can't escape it. It is coming, unless I greatly mistake symptoms!" he muttered, as he went out.

Percy remained in his room until the afternoon, then he set forth upon a visit to Centerville; and in the excitement of the hour, and under the stimulating effect of Dr. Sydney's tonic, he felt himself wonderfully improved as he walked up the village street.

He went directly to Helena. He had resolved to tell her the whole story, and abide by her decision of what was right for him to do.

"She has no actual knowledge of the world," he said to himself; "but she is endowed with divine wisdom, broad sympathies, and a natural understanding of the human heart. She is my best adviser."

She held out her hand to him, when she came into the room, saying: "This is an unexpected pleasure, Mr. Durand."

But he did not take the proffered hand. He only answered: "Wait. I came here to make a confession to you, and to ask your advice. Perhaps, after you have heard my story, you will not want to clasp my hand."

She looked up at him, startled, wondering.

"Surely you have not committed murder!" she said. "You do not resemble an assassin, Mr. Durand."

"There are different degrees of murder," he replied, "and I think to murder a human heart is the cruelest of all."

"Have you done that willfully?" she asked, lifting her sombre eyes to his face. "Then, indeed, I will not offer you my hand in greeting."

"No, no!" he added hastily, "not willfully, but thoughtlessly! and thoughtlessness is the consort of selfishness, and the two are parents of crime. But now listen to my story, Miss Maxon. I will be brief."

"My father died when I was but a child, and left me the only heir to an independent fortune. I grew into early manhood with this knowledge, a sad knowledge for any youth, because it leaves him with the consciousness that he need not exert his own powers of brain or muscle to make a name and place in Society. My mother died when I was fifteen, just at the time I most needed her gentle counsels, and refining influence. I was selfish, proud, passionate, strong-willed. But I tried to make a man of myself for the sake of my mother's memory. I believed all women were saints, because she was one. At twenty I met a beautiful woman, two or three years my senior. She possessed a magnificent form, and a face of wonderful brunette beauty. Every man in my circle was raving over her, and I became madly infatuated. I asked her to be my wife and she consented. I reveled in dreams of a home, something I had not known since my mother died. A few days before the time set for our wedding, I discovered that the woman I worshiped was making sport of me, and that she had promised to be my wife only to secure my fortune. More shocking still, she was carrying on the most flagrant infidelities, which were the talk of the club-rooms, while I, poor dupe, only discovered the horrible truth at the last hour. I was but a youth, and this experience nearly wrecked my life.

"I lost faith in everything, human and divine, for a time. As years passed my wound healed, but all my views of life were changed. I looked upon women as vain, frivolous and deceitful, and whatever amusement they could afford me, I considered myself justified in taking. Marriage seemed to me a bondage, and love a dream sure to end in misery: a dream which could never disturb my heart again.

"After years of travel, adventure and folly, when a wearisome ennui toward the whole world had taken possession of me, I met a lovely woman.

"She also abhorred marriage, and had sworn eternal warfare against it. She was more pronounced and bitter in her denunciations of the social system than I. She was a charming companion; but I felt that the association was dangerous, and tried to fly from it. A perverse fate, however, constantly threw us together. Finally, she was left entirely alone in the world. In an evil hour, when she was weeping because her life was so desolate, I asked her to decide between the society she despised, and my companionship and protection."

He paused. It was hard to go on with those truthful, earnest, pure eyes gazing at him. How could he make her understand?

"Well, and what was her answer?" Helena asked, almost in a whisper.

"She has been living in pleasant apartments in New York, as my friend and comrade, for almost two years. Do you understand?"

"I understand," she answered, and a sudden chill shook her from head to foot.

"We were very happy for a year, for longer," he went on, hurriedly. "She was perfectly happy, because she believed she was doing right. I was not as happy as I had expected to be. My conscience seemed often to cry out, after years of silence; but I would not listen to it. We passed many delightful hours together, and I was always proud to think my friend was a beautiful, refined and true woman. I congratulated myself, that at least, I had shown better taste in the selection of my companion, than many of my friends who were similarly situated. The lady was independently wealthy, and our association was prompted by congenial tastes and affection.

"Then I met you. Your voice woke all the higher impulses of my nature: your conversation lifted me into a strangely rarified atmosphere; I abhorred my old life from the hour I met you. I have tried to break away from it, but I cannot without crushing a human heart. Unfortunately, my friend has passed through no such change of feeling. She is happy, and she loves me. To leave her alone, to desert her, seems heartless and cruel. The way of escape is hedged about with unforeseen difficulties. I am tortured from within and without. Surely the way of the transgressor is hard. I would reform my life, if I knew how. Can you tell me what is right to do under the circumstances?"

She was very pale. Her hands were clasped tightly before her. Her breath came hard. "There is one way, only one," she said. "I wonder it has not suggested itself to you. Make the tie that binds you to your friend a legal one. Make her your wife, and let the future atone for the past."

He started to his feet as if she had struck him.

"It is impossible!" he said. "She would never consent. It is opposed to all her theories."

Helena looked at him coldly, a dumb pain in her face.

"I fear you cannot understand our very peculiar situation," he went on. "But you must believe I am telling you the whole truth. I am not misstating one thing. There has been no effort at misleading this woman, this friend of mine. There never was any talk of marriage between us, save to condemn it. She often said she liked me first, because I did not endeavor to convert her from her pet theories, as many men had done. She is very beautiful, and has been annoyed by many suitors. But she is almost a monomaniac upon the subject. You would find less to condemn in my course, if you could understand how peculiar and deep-rooted were her prejudices."

"I do understand," Helena answered. "I once knew just such a person as you describe. We were school-mates, and she shocked us all on graduating day, by an anti-marriage address. So I can understand the type of woman you describe. Yet these views of hers did not necessitate the grave course of action you suggested to her later on, surely."

Percy flushed. "No," he said, "that was the result of our dangerous companionship, and my selfishness. I could not continue in the platonic association so satisfactory to her, and I could not give her up easily, and so the great mistake was made. The error of a lifetime is often committed in a moment, you know. And now"

"And now," Helena continued, calmly, with white lips as he paused, "now the right course of action for you seems very clearly defined. You can at least tell her of your changed ideas, and offer her marriage. If she declines, you are justified in leaving her. She has no right to compel you to live an unprincipled life. But she will not decline your offer. Even Heloise yielded her opinions and liberal theories to the request of Abelard, and became his wife, you know."

Percy had been walking the room excitedly while she spoke. As she ceased, he turned, and stood facing her with his arms folded.

"There is one more thing to tell you," he said. "Something which renders the advice you give impossible for me to follow. I love another woman with all the fervor of my soul, with all the strength of my heart. Love her with a love that lifts me up to the very gates of heaven, and purifies my whole nature like a refining fire. I see her face, waking or sleeping. I hear her voice in the silence of the night, and above the roar of the street, by day. It is a love which only comes to one man in a thousand, because only one woman in a million can inspire it. This love is at once an agony and a rapture. It asks, it expects no return. It fills my life full here, and it will pervade eternity for me when I die. But, loving like this, even though hopelessly, it would be sacrilege to ask any other woman to be my wife. Even to right a wrong, one should not commit a greater wrong, that of sinning against the holiest and most sacred emotion which ever entered a human heart."

While he spoke, Helena had grown crimson from brow to chin. Then she turned deathly pale, and, burying her face in her hands, she sank into a chair, sobbing wildly.

When he had told her the story of his life, she had wondered at the terrible pain it gave her to listen. But she had believed it was the disappointment she felt in finding her ideal friend so earthly. This together with her sympathy for the unknown woman.

Now, as she listened to his strangely impassioned words, there came to her a revelation that she had given him all the pent-up passion of her soul, all the pure love of her woman's heart. And to what end? The knowledge startled, shocked and terrified her, and she sobbed like a frightened child.

Percy was unmanned at the sight of her tears, yet this unexpected outburst filled him with sudden hope. After all, this divine being, this goddess did love him. He forgot everything, save that one fact.

"Helena!" he cried, kneeling before her, and striving to uncover her face, "my darling, my queen, look at me, speak to me."

She pushed him from her, and rose hurriedly.

"Oh!" she sobbed, "you are cruel. Do you want to break two hearts!" Then, as if alarmed at her own words, she added quickly, "You must go away now and leave me. I am all unnerved, I can not give you any more advice to-day. Please go." But as he turned to obey her, she called him back.

"One word only I would say to you now. Do not tell your friend, what you have told me. Do not tell her that you love another woman. It will be hard enough for her to know that you are to go out of her life, without having that bitter knowledge added."

"God bless you!" he cried, his eyes full of tears. "You are the most generous woman I ever dreamed of in my wildest visions of what was noble."

Even in the supreme hour of her own new found misery, a misery so vast it seemed to fill the whole earth, Helena thought of her rival and tried to save her pain. Truly had Percy said she was one woman in a million.

CHAPTER XX. THE HARVEST OF TARES

Percy returned to the Hotel, and before taking the train for New York, he wrote Helena a letter. Its contents were as follows:

"MY QUEEN:

"All my life I have worshiped an ideal. Just when I had grown to believe, that she did not exist save in my dreams, you flashed upon my horizon. I loved you; but I have not dared dream that you would love me, until to-day. I saw it in your face, dear, and I know that you are a woman who, once loving, will love forever. You know the story of my life. I am going abroad very soon. I shall remain away, until this miserable experience of which I told you, this terrible error, becomes a thing of the past. I shall strive to make myself worthy of your respect, of your love. When I come back, I shall ask you to be my wife, Helena. Until then, farewell. Read the verses I enclose. I found them in the poet's corner of one of our daily papers, and cut them out, because they seemed like a versified history of my own life. First, the mirage dream, then the jungle of the senses, then the cold world of fashion, until I lost faith in the existence of the storied Land of Love.

"Then I met you, and you taught me that the true kingdom of love lies in the precincts of a pure home. Farewell, my sweet saint, my angel guide.

"PERCY DURAND."

The poem he enclosed we give below.

THE KINGDOM OF LOVE.

In the dawn of the day, when the sea and the earth Reflected the sunrise above, I set forth, with a heart full of courage and mirth, To seek for the Kingdom of Love. I asked of a Poet I met on the way, Which cross-road would lead me aright. And he said: "Follow me, and ere long you will see Its glistening turrets of Light."

And soon in the distance a city shone fair; "Look yonder," he said, "there it gleams!" But alas! for the hopes that were doomed to despair, It was only the Kingdom of Dreams. Then the next man I asked was a gay cavalier, And he said: "Follow me, follow me," And with laughter and song we went speeding along By the shores of life's beautiful sea,

Till we came to a valley more tropical far, Than the wonderful Vale of Cashmere. And I saw from a bower a face like a flower, Smile out on the gay cavalier. And he said: "We have come to humanity's goal. Here love and delight are intense." But alas! and alas! for the hope of my soul. It was only the Kingdom of Sense.

As I journeyed more slowly, I met on the road, A coach with retainers behind, And they said: "Follow us, for our lady's abode Belongs in the realm you would find." 'Twas a grand dame of fashion, a newly-wed bride; I followed, encouraged and bold. But my hopes died away, like the last gleams of day, For we came to the Kingdom of Gold.

At the door of a cottage I asked a fair maid. "I have heard of that Realm," she replied, "But my feet never roam from the Kingdom of Home, So I know not the way," and she sighed. I looked on the cottage, how restful it seemed! And the maid was as fair as a dove. Great light glorified my soul as I cried, "Why, home is the Kingdom of Love!"

The following day, when Percy ushered himself into Dolores' apartments by his latch-key, he was surprised to find those bijou rooms in a state of disorder. Boxes, trunks, and packing cases were scattered about, while Dolores, attired in a loose white gown, was busily at work arranging garments and bric-a-brac.

"What in the world are you doing?" he asked, in amazement. "Are you going away?"

She lifted her wan, white face to his, with a look so pathetic, so full of widowed sorrow, that his heart smote him. O, Sin! how bitter are thy fruits.

"Yes, I am going away," she said. "Come and sit down here, and let me tell you all about it." And she led him to his favorite chair and sank upon the ottoman at his feet. "Ever since you went away the last time, I have been thinking, thinking, thinking," she said, pressing her hands to her head, "until I nearly grew wild. And the result of it all is, that I am going away: going to California. I think it is better that we should be parted, at least for a time."

She looked eagerly in his face; somehow she had fancied that when he found she was really determined to go away from him, that his old love for her, and his longing for her companionship would overmaster every other consideration.

She had reasoned it all out, through the sleepless night.

"He will be surprised, startled and hurt," she thought. "He does not believe I have strength to leave him. But I will go and he shall follow me and sue hard, before I return to him. Not until I am gone will he fully realize what my love has been to him. If I were his wife, now, I could not go, and he would know I could not. When he stops and thinks what this step might mean and all it might mean, I know he will regret having driven me to it. Even if he has tired of me himself, man-like, he will dread the possibility of my going to another lover, as many women in my situation would do. But go where I will I shall be true to him, oh, so true! for I must love him, and him only till I die. It is my fate."

So she had talked to herself while she made her plans. Now, when she had told him that she was going away, she looked up in his face, expecting to see surprise and chagrin. Instead, she saw only relief, intense relief.

"Yes, Dolores, it is better that we should part, even as you say," he answered. "There is a better and a truer life for each of us, than the life we are living, even if it is a lonelier one. We have made a great mistake, but we can rectify it in a measure, by parting now."

All hope died in her heart. Her face flushed, her breast heaved with violent emotion.

"You are late in finding this out!" she said, bitterly; "but I believe it is customary with men, to never discover mistakes of this kind, until the woman's life is wrecked. It is so very natural for a man to moralize standing on a crushed and ruined heart."

"Dolores, let us part without any bitter words, for heaven's sake!" he cried. "Our mistake, our sin, whatever we may choose to call it, has been mutual. I never lured you to destruction; I never deceived you; I never meant to wrong you. You understood the world, you were no ignorant girl: you were a woman, old enough to know the importance of the step I proposed."

"Had I been a young girl I should never have yielded," she answered. "It is the ripe fruit which falls when a south wind shakes the tree."

"Well, you must not forget that we agreed upon the course of action which has resulted in our misery. Neither should blame the other. Let us part friends, not enemies."

"Friends!" and all of wounded pride and scorned love, and hopeless passion was in her voice as she repeated the word.

Ah! when will a man ever learn that he cannot offer a more cruel insult to a woman he has once professed to love, than to call her his "friend."

Percy felt great drops of perspiration starting out on his brow. He drew his handkerchief from his pocket, and with it a letter fluttered and fell at Dolores' feet.

She picked it up, and she might have returned it without a glance at the superscription had not Percy sprung forward with a guilty flush, crying hurriedly,

"Excuse my awkwardness; give me the letter, please?"

Then she glanced down upon it. It was addressed in a delicate feminine penmanship, and the date of the post-mark was not a week old.

A sudden suspicion fired her blood; her pansy eyes blazed black as sloes as she turned them on Percy's tell-tale face.

"So!" she said, slowly and mockingly; "there is a cause for all this excess of morality, mon ami, is there?"

"Give me the letter, please?" was his only response.

She took a step back, and looked at him with defiant eyes.

"I demand to know the contents of this letter before I return it!" she said. "If it in no way relates to our proposed separation, you will not fear to show it to me. If it does, I have a right to know."

He looked at her coldly, and his words, as they fell, pierced her like poisoned arrows.

"You have no right to demand any thing of the kind," he said, quietly. "Our relations are simply with each other. We have always understood that, I believe. You are not that most despised object in your own eyes, Dolores, a wife. Therefore you have no right to question me concerning my correspondence. The letter, please."

She threw it at his feet. "Take it!" she cried, "but remember, Percy Durand, as God hears me, no other woman shall be your wife while I live."

He turned toward the door without a word. But as he went, he took her latch-key from his pocket and dropped it carelessly on the open leaf of her ebony desk.

That one act, said more effectually than the bitterest words could have said, that all was at an end between them. He was no longer her comrade, her friend, her lover, who came and went at will; he was a stranger, who, if he ever came again, would come in the capacity of a guest.

She flung out her arms with a wild cry:

"Percy, Percy, come back! Do not leave me like this, I cannot bear it."

He turned back, moved by the passionate pain of her voice.

As he turned, his eye fell upon an old photograph, lying among a parcel of letters, in the open tray of a partially packed trunk.

"Who is this, Dolores?" he asked, picking up the card, and standing as if transfixed.

Dolores went forward and looked over his shoulder. She thought he was relenting toward her, and if a reconciliation seemed possible, she desired it at any cost.

Ah! pitying heaven! how at the mercy of the weakest man, the strongest woman is, if she loves him.

"That?" she said, laying her hand gently on his arm, "that is an old picture of a school-mate of mine, oh, how long ago it seems! She was the only intimate friend I ever had until I met Mrs. Butler. And yet I have utterly lost all trace of her. Our correspondence died a natural death, before I had been two years abroad."

"What was her name?" asked Percy, and his heart almost stood still to listen to her reply.

"Her name was Lena, Helena Maxon. She lived in a pretty place called Elm Hill. I suppose she is married and the mother of a family ere this. She was just the kind of girl to marry young, and she was abnormally fond of babies, I remember. She actually brought her doll to school with her, when she was seventeen years old."

Dolores talked on volubly, glad to forget the torturing scene of a few moments before. She fancied that he felt the same, and that he was asking these questions simply to bridge over their quarrel.

Percy thought the room was whirling around him. He sat down in a neighboring chair.

"I wonder you never spoke of her to me before!" he said. "She has an interesting face. I did not know you had such a friend in America. Why have you never looked her up?"

She gazed at him in questioning surprise, his voice, his manner were so strange.

"I think I mentioned her to you when I told you the story of my Uncle's death," she answered, pleasantly, eager to win him to good humor again. "While abroad, our lives drifted so far apart, I seldom recalled the old intimacy. Since my return, I have hardly felt situated to seek a renewal of our acquaintance. It might have been embarrassing for both of us, Percy, and you know I have not felt the need of any friend or companion but you."

He laid down the picture and covered his eyes as if to shut out the sight of it.

"My God!" he cried, suddenly, "it cannot be true, it is too terrible."

Dolores' jealous suspicions concerning the letter took definite shape and form.

"Why are you talking so strangely?" she asked, facing him suddenly. "Do you know Helena Maxon, Percy? Have you ever met her?"

"Yes," he answered, "I know her, I have met her. Oh, Dolores, I wish to God I were dead."

"I wish we both were!" she cried passionately. "I wish God had sent death to us there in that Andean valley, when something told me, that we were never to be so happy again." Then, growing excited, she clenched her slender hands and stood before him, speaking in a low suppressed voice. "You shall never marry her, never!" she cried. "I can hinder it. When we were in Santiago, you registered me as your wife, to avoid gossip. To Lorette, you have called me Madame Percy, your wife. These things, told in a court of justice, would prevent you from making another woman your wife. I will follow you to the ends of the earth to prevent it."

Percy put his hands to his head in a dazed way.

"Don't!" he protested wearily. "I am ill, suffering, Dolores. Let us end this miserable scene. I have no idea of making any woman my wife. It would be an insult to any good woman to ask her to take the remnant of my miserable existence.

"I am going abroad at once, to-morrow; and I hope you will continue your preparations for your journey. And now, good by, I am too ill to endure another word to-day."

He loosened the hold she had taken on his arm in her excitement, and almost staggered out of the room and down the stairs.

CHAPTER XXI. A STRANGE MARRIAGE

When Percy returned to his apartments he found a letter from Helena awaiting him. It was written in reply to his, posted to her before leaving Centerville.

His head was aching, and his vision blurred strangely as he read the written words. It began without an address, abruptly.

"I, too, have worshiped an ideal all my life. A man without reproach, and above dishonor. A man strong in all manly attributes, strong in his loves and his emotions, but strong, too, in his pride, and in his will power. I think God never bestows the one without the other; but man too often cultivates the former and leaves the latter unused. For the ideal I so worshiped, I kept my heart free and my soul unsullied. When you came, all unconsciously I invested you with the attributes of my ideal. All unconsciously, until too late to place a guard upon my unwise heart, it poured out its long-hidden treasures. So suddenly the knowledge came upon me, that I betrayed to you what had been wiser to conceal. Wiser, because added to the Creator's uneven distribution of pains and penalties, the world bestows its merciless condemnation upon the woman who reveals that which is so difficult to hide.

God formed man and woman out of the self-same clay! breathed into their bodies the self-same breath of life, endowed them with the self-same human nature. But a civilized Society permits man to exult in a display of the emotions which it demands that woman shall mask or deny.

Upon the weaker being devolves the double duty of fighting against the aggressive impulses of the stronger, while she controls her own.

She who fails to do this, loses the esteem of the man who has awakened the slumbering passions of her heart.

That I love you, I will not attempt to deny. I think God meant us for each other in the beginning. But I give much to the man I love, when I give myself, penniless and nameless though I am, I give a whole heart, untouched by any belittling half-loves or debasing jealousies. While I have waited for the coming of the King, I have allowed no pretender to occupy the throne in my heart, even for an hour. I have given no man on earth the right to think I loved him, until you came. No man exists who can point his hand at me and say, 'we were lovers once.' Has not she who gives a stainless womanhood, a pure, wholesome body, and a true, warm heart, the right to demand much in return? She either undervalues her own worth, or overvalues the worth of any man, it seems to me, who does not demand it.

And yet, knowing the story of your life, in all its tragic details, its temptations, and its trials, I have felt to-day many times, that I loved as deeply or as unwisely as other women have loved, loved enough to find my happiness in reforming the object of my affections. Let no man consider this a woman's true sphere. If, out of the vastness of her love, she is willing to lean down to him, let him bow in reverence before her: not lightly taking it as her duty and his right.

But while I love you, and must love you forever, even as you have said, I can never be your wife.

I cannot lead you into your newly-found Kingdom of Love, when by so doing I must tread upon another woman's bleeding heart. I could not accept happiness bought at the price of another's misery and despair.

Over the fairest day the future could prepare for us, there would always hang the shadow of another's life-long sorrow.

Could I answer you otherwise, under the circumstances, I would not be worthy of your love. Yet, if I did not know that this life is only a very small portion of our existence, I might be so mad with selfish passion that I should forget every consideration save my love for you.

But I believe that those who belong to each other spiritually will find each other and dwell together through eternities of love.

I believe we shall. But while here, on earth, we must make ourselves worthy of that life, by unselfish thoughtfulness of others, by self-denial, and suffering, if need be. You have made a terrible mistake, which can only be atoned for by a life of repentance and resolve. And I must suffer with you. The great wrong, in a mistake or a sin like yours, is that it reaches out and injures those who are guiltless. Two people make laws unto themselves and say, 'It is no one's business, we wrong no one save ourselves.' Yet invariably others are eventually wronged.

No soul ever transgressed a divine law of morality, without injuring some innocent being.

There is no absolute individuality. We are all linked and lashed together by invisible but indestructible threads, spun down from the Great Source. When any man attempts to extricate himself from others and stand alone, a guide and god unto himself, he but more hopelessly interlaces and snarls the web which unites us all.

You, my friend, have snarled the threads about us: but even in my pain there lies a joy in the consciousness that I suffer through, and with you. It is sweeter than to rejoice with another. In the beginning of time, God married our souls; that we are separated during one brief stage of existence cannot hinder our final eternal union. Be true to your new self, and 'run your race in patience, for you are surrounded by a cloud of witnesses.' God bless you, and adieu.

"HELENA."

A chill that seemed to shake the marrow in his bones and the core in his heart, seized upon Percy as he laid the letter down. He disrobed as quickly as possible, and rolled himself up in the covers of his warm bed, but he felt as if he were packed in ice, despite all his efforts, until the return of the fever set his veins on fire.

Dr. Sydney smiled grimly, with an "I told you so" expression, when he again stood by Percy's bed-side. But Percy did not wait to hear his accusing words.

"I have resigned myself to my fate, you see, doctor," he said, "and I am convinced that you know more than I do. I think I am going to be very sick; and I want you to tell me the exact truth about myself, as I have some very important directions to leave concerning my affairs, if there is the least hope of my death."

"Hope!" echoed Dr. Sydney, "Tut, tut, man, what are you talking in that vein for, a young, handsome, fortunate fellow like you, with all your life before you?"

Percy smiled sadly.

"My life is all behind me, unfortunately, Doctor," he said. "At least the best opportunities of it are, and they lie among tares, lost in a rank growth of wild oats. It is all very well to say that every man must plant that crop, but I realize when too late that I must reap the harvest as well; and it has filled my store-house so full, there is no room for one golden sheaf of wheat."

"Might thresh your wheat then, in the stack, and sell it without storing it," suggested the old doctor, facetiously, as he held Percy's pulse between his thumb and finger. "Fall wheat brings good prices now. H'm! pretty high fever, how's your tongue?"

"Pretty sick, pretty sick, my boy!" he said, as he finished his examination. "Liver in an awful state. That's what makes you want to die, and all that. A diseased liver and melancholy views of life are as natural companions as a boy and a piece of string. If you don't object, I'll call counsel?"

Percy looked up quickly.

"Then I am in danger?"

"Possibly, not positively. I see indications that lead me to think an abcess is forming on your liver. But I am not sure of it."

"In case there is?"

"In case there is, you will have to submit to an operation."

"And such operations are often fatal, are they not, in their results? Frequently so."

Dr. Sydney hesitated.

"They are sometimes fatal," he said. "You would require skillful treatment, and careful nursing. I must obtain a good nurse for you, at once, and I would like to call in Dr. Manville."

Dr. Manville, after a thorough examination, and diagnosis of the case, agreed with Dr. Sydney in relation to the symptoms of the disease.

"They are obscure, and it is at this time difficult to locate the abcess," he said to Percy, who insisted upon knowing his exact condition. "But I am convinced that an operation must take place before long. Your case is serious; and I would advise you to send for your relatives."

Percy shook his head sadly.

"I have only one relative in the world," he said, "and she is now in Europe with her husband and children. But I have friends I wish to send for at once. Will you kindly give me the utensils to write out a telegram, Doctor?"

The telegram, when completed, was addressed to "Mr. Thomas Griffith, Centerville, N. Y.," and read: "Come at once. Bring your wife and Helena. A matter of life and death." Then followed his name and address.

A few hours later, they came, startled, wondering, anxious. Dr. Sydney was alone with the patient, awaiting the arrival of the nurse. He ushered the pale trio to Percy's bed-side, and was about to retire to an adjoining room, when Percy detained him.

"Wait!" he said. "I want you to tell my friends, Doctor, my exact condition, just as you have told me. Spare nothing."

Dr. Sydney did as Percy requested. "And now," added Percy, "I wish to say for myself that I have no expectations of recovery. I do not want to live, and I shall make no effort to assist my medical advisers in restoring me to health. And since I must die, Helena, let me make you my wife. Let me leave you the lawful heir of my otherwise useless wealth, and let your hands minister to my last wants while on earth. It will not be long; but that brief time will be rendered the happiest of my whole life, if I can have your care, and companionship. Helena will you not consent?"

Mrs. Griffith was sobbing and Mr. Griffith and Dr. Sydney were wiping their eyes.

Helena alone was tearless. But her heart seemed dying within her, so sudden, so terrible, so unexpected was this situation.

"Helena, will you consent?" Percy repeated.

"I cannot, oh, I cannot!" she cried.

"Helena!" It was Mrs. Griffith who spoke now through her sobs. "Helena, you are cruel. Don't you know it is a dying man you are refusing to make happy upon his death-bed?"

"There may be one chance for his life, and you are ruining that. It is murder!" Mr. Griffith added.

"He needs some tender woman's care, he must have it!" said the Doctor. "No money can buy the kind of care and nursing he needs during the next month or six weeks."

Helena put her hands to her temple, with a distracted gesture. "Oh, you do not any of you understand!" she cried; "it is not my place, Percy, may I see you alone a moment?"

"H'm, h'm! quite a romance here!" mused Dr. Sydney, as he trotted out of the room with his hands clasped under his coat-tails. "Liver trouble and love affairs together, bad complication, very bad. Enough to pull any man down. Hope the girl will marry him and nurse him. She has the look of a born mother in her face. Some women have. They always make good nurses."

Meanwhile, Helena was kneeling by Percy's bed-side, her hands clasping his, her face luminous with love and her heart torn with conflicting emotions.

"Oh, my darling, my darling!" she cried, passionately, "it is not that I do not love you enough to forgive all that has occurred, in this solemn hour, and devote myself to your care. But I think of her, you have belonged to her, she has loved you and shared your life; and now, to come suddenly forward, to displace her, to take your name, your fortune, and the sad, sacred duty of ministering to perhaps your last wants on earth, oh, it seems cruel, heartless! It is her right, not mine."

"And now listen to me quietly," Percy answered, as he stroked her hair gently. "She whom you mention is not within call, even if I desired her presence. When I returned from Centerville, I found her all packed to go to California. I bade her adieu, with the understanding that it was our last farewell, and she supposes me now preparing for a trip to Europe. She does not need my fortune, and she never desired my name. I shall die happier to bestow both on you. If I believed there remained one possibility of recovery for me, I would never ask you to be my wife, Helena. I am not, I never can be worthy of you here. But I think I shall make greater progress in the spirit world, and be better fitted to journey on beside you there, if I die knowing you are my wife. Will you consent, Helena?"

"I will," she said, solemnly; and leaned her face, wet now with tears, upon his breast. And that was their betrothal.

Then, as gently as he could, he told her of the strange discovery he had made during his last interview with Dolores: a discovery Helena's clairvoyant perceptions had already half divined. From the hour he first told her his story, she had constantly associated his unknown and unnamed friend with the thought of Dolores.

Though bitter and painful the actual knowledge of the truth, she was yet spared the ordeal of a stunning surprise as she listened to his revelation.

An hour later, the always solemn and now doubly-impressive marriage service was responded to by a bride clothed all in black, and a pallid groom lying upon his death-bed.

Scarcely was the ceremony concluded, when Percy was seized by a violent chill, followed by intense pain, and other alarming symptoms. The morning found him greatly reduced in strength, and unable to move upon the pillow without a groan of agony; throughout the day he grew rapidly worse, and every hope of ultimate recovery was abandoned.

"I doubt if he lives to endure the operation which must take place shortly," Dr. Sydney said to Mr. Griffith in the afternoon, as he paused by the door before descending the stairs. "He has passed through too much mental excitement during the last twenty-four hours. He has developed most alarming symptoms since midnight, which complicate the case seriously. Permit no one to see him to-day; leave this door open occasionally to allow circulation of fresh air."

As he turned to go, a boy in messenger's costume, presented himself at the door. "Message for Mr. Durand," he said, smartly. "Thirty cents due."

Dr. Sydney gave the boy a slight push.

"Go along with you," he growled. "Mr. Durand is sick, he may not live till morning. Go tell your employer not to bother us at such a time with messages."

The boy hurried away, as if frightened at the close proximity of death to the locality.

"I shall call again this evening," Dr. Sydney added, as he went slowly down the stairs; and then he muttered to himself: "A serious case, a serious case."

CHAPTER XXII. DEAD IN HER BED.

As the door closed upon Percy after that tragic interview, Dolores stood and listened to his departing footsteps, until the last echo died away.

Then she flung herself down among the objects which were all associated with their happy hours of love and companionship, while dry despairing sobs shook her frail form.

"Oh, Christ, pity me! my life is all in ruins, all in ruins!" she moaned, "Father, Mother, God, why did you curse me with the existence I never desired?"

After a time, she rose up and tried to set her apartment in order. Every where she turned her eyes, they were greeted with some reminder of her life with Percy. Here was a souvenir of the happy bohemian days, in Paris. There a momento of that fatal ice-boat journey. Fatal, because she believed it was during that dangerous experience that Mrs. Butler contracted the illness which resulted in her death; and because on that day, Percy really passed from the position of friend to lover. Then, as she opened a book, trying to divert her tortured mind from these memories, out dropped a pressed fern, gathered in the Andean valley. She covered her face with her hands; she seemed to see again the fading glory of that wonderful sunset, the towering steeples of granite, and again she could hear the saucy Ta-ha-ha of the arajojo bird.

It was more than she could bear. She rose hurriedly, and walked across the room, weeping silently.

Suddenly her eyes fell upon the old faded photograph, which Percy had dropped beside the chair he occupied. She picked it up and gazed upon it with passionate fury, distorting her beautiful face.

"Curse you, curse you!" she almost shrieked, and tearing the card in a thousand fragments, she trampled them under her feet, and fell in a dead swoon upon the floor beside them.

It was dark when she returned to consciousness. She groped her way toward her couch, and, throwing herself upon it, fell into a troubled sleep, which lasted until the entrance of Lorette the following day.

She awoke to renewed suffering, and spent wretched hours in forming a thousand futile plans of revenge. Scarcely having tasted food since Percy's departure, she felt her strength leaving her. And with her strength, went her anger, resentment and pride. During the long sleepless night, of the second day, the desire to see Percy again overmastered every other feeling. The intensity of her love seemed to increase, as her physical vigor lessened. The knowledge that, no matter how she destroyed his happiness, or ruined his hopes in life, she must still love him, and live without him, bore down upon her heart like a burning weight, and put to flight all desire for revenge. The one thing, the only thing which made the future worth living, was a reconciliation with Percy.

She rose and sat by her window in the chill, gray dawn.

"He must come back to me, he must," she whispered, "at any cost! I have given up the whole world for his love, for his companionship. Even if his love has been given to another, he must still give me his companionship. I will see him, I will send for him to-day, and tell him so."

A strange idea had presented itself to her feverish, suffering heart. An idea born of her wild love and her crushed and ruined pride. In the silent watches of the night, the thought had come to her, that even if Percy made Helena his wife, he might still give her (his comrade, his long-time confidant and friend) his occasional affectionate companionship. If she submitted quietly and passively to his marriage, he might not wholly cast her off. She believed that society was full of men, respectable citizens in the eyes of the world, who retained their intimate lady friends after marriage. And she knew that the United States Government permitted a large and increasing colony to exist, where men retained any number of wives.

Surely, if any woman on earth had the right to be so retained, it was she. And Percy would see it so, and he would not cast her off. She could scarcely wait for the day to advance, to send for him and lay the plan before him.

She had not the faintest comprehension of the mighty magnitude or the exalted nature of the love which had sprung to life in Percy's heart for Helena. She believed it to be the passing fancy of the hour, a sudden passion of the senses. She remembered the subtle magnetism which Helena possessed in days of old, a peculiar power of drawing people to her, of attracting them and winning their confidence with no seeming effort of her own. She remembered how popular she was in Madame Scranton's Academy and in those days she had believed it to be the mesmerism of her eyes, that won the hearts of her companions. Percy was, no doubt, affected by this mysterious influence which fascinated everyone who lingered long in Helena's presence. But it would pass away, and his love for her, his ideal mate and comrade, would burn again with greater lustre, if she waited patiently.

She wrote a note, full of humility, begging his forgiveness for her conduct during their last interview, and asking him to grant her a few moments' conversation during the day. She sent for a messenger to carry the note, and then she dismissed Lorette for the day and began to prepare herself for the expected guest.

Lorette took her departure reluctantly. "Madame is not herself; Madame is ill, and needs looking after!" she muttered, as she went out, and many times during the day and in succeeding days and weeks, her light volatile French spirits were shadowed by the recollection of her mistress's face, as she last saw it.

Dolores was one of the few women who can be beautiful even when suffering mental and physical pain. As a rule, happiness and health are necessary cosmetics to beauty; but hers was a face that even much weeping, and sleepless nights of torturing pain could not disfigure.

She robed herself all in white, as Percy best loved to see her. She wore his favorite jewels, and a bright knot of ribbon he had once admired, at her throat. Suddenly, in the midst of her preparation, she paused. The full consciousness of her humiliating position dawned upon her with startling force.

"My God! how low I have fallen!" she sobbed, and yet she did not draw back from the resolution she had formed, to throw herself upon the pity of the man she loved.

She had been Queen of the feast; and now she was about to beg for crumbs from the table presided over by another.

The hours lagged by on leaden wings. Why did not the messenger return?

It was late in the afternoon when he made his appearance. He was out of breath from running up the flight of stairs, and he handed her back, her own note.

"Could you not find the gentleman? I told you to leave the note if he was not in!" she said sharply, so keen was her disappointment.

"Yes'm, I know you did," the boy answered, "but there was people there, and a doctor. And the doctor he came to the door, and he said as the gentleman mustn't be disturbed, he was sick, and goin' to die before mornin', perhaps. And I felt scared like, and come off without leaving the letter."

The boy turned away, and Dolores closed the door upon him, quickly, as if to shut out his evil message with him.

Sick, dying! and who were the people with him? who had the right to be with him and minister to his needs, save herself? It was her place, hers only. She must go to him, she must save him by the strength of her love.

She did not wait to make any change in her attire. She seized the nearest garment at hand, a soft white shawl, and a hat with nodding white plumes, and hurried forth.

When she reached the building in which Percy's apartments were situated, she met the physician just emerging from the street door. She forced a calm exterior as she addressed him.

"I came to ask after your patient," she said. "Is it true that he is not expected to live?"

He looked at her sharply. Her white attire, her beauty and her pallor made her a remarkable picture as she stood there in the gathering dusk.

"Are you a relative of his?" he asked.

She shook her head. "No, only a friend; one to whom he has been very kind," she answered. "But I want you to tell me the truth. Will he die?"

"I fear he will," the old physician answered, gravely. "There is small chance that he can live through the night. If he lives, it will be a miracle." Then he passed on.

She glided through the entrance he had left open, and hurried up the flight of stairs that led to his rooms. The door stood ajar upon the landing. She pushed it open and entered; no one was visible in the outer room which served as a parlor. At one side, in a sort of study, sat a gentleman and lady engaged in low conversation; but they did not hear her light footsteps as she walked across the yielding carpet, and stood between the velvet portieres which curtained his sleeping-room.

Through the colored globe the gas-light shone with subdued lustre, filling the apartment with the mellow halo of an autumn sunset.

Propped up on pillows lay Percy, while above him leaned the shapely figure of a woman clothed all in black; her dusky hair and brunette face showing in marked contrast to the blond locks and marble pallor of the patient.

Her hand was making light soothing passes across his brow; her eyes were full of unutterable love and sorrow. Gently she drooped over his pillow and pressed a light kiss upon his closed lids, as she murmured, "My love, my husband."

Dolores drew a deep, gasping breath, like one who has been struck suddenly by an unseen foe.

Helena heard the sound, and turned a startled glance in the direction from which it came.

Standing between the velvet curtains, she saw the motionless figure of Dolores, majestic in her beauty, her white garments and her golden hair clearly defined against the crimson background of the draperies.

Just for one breathless, pained second the two women who had been schoolmates and dear friends, looked into each other's eyes again. Then, as Helena made a movement toward her, Dolores turned her glance upon Percy, a strange, radiant, triumphant smile illuminating her face, and vanished as suddenly as she had appeared.

As she made her way through the city streets, many turned to look upon the white-robed figure, and the strangely-beautiful smiling face under the nodding plumes of her hat. But no man dared speak to her. There was something in her face that awed them, and protected her from insult.

She was still smiling when she entered her own apartment again. Carefully laying aside her wraps, she proceeded to set the room in perfect order. Then she brought out a little ebony box, in which she kept many curious souvenirs of her life abroad. In one corner lay a small chamois-skin bag. She opened it, and into a corner of a snowy cambric handkerchief, she shook a portion of its contents, a brilliant, crystallized substance, and then replaced the bag and locked the ebony box away in her cabinet again.

Laying the handkerchief on the pillow of her couch, she disrobed, brushed out her beautiful hair, and leaving the gas jet turned low, she crept into her snowy bed. Bringing the handkerchief close to her face, she looked smilingly down on the tiny crystals of the powder, as she murmured, "If only Madame Volkenburg was not mistaken, if only it is swift and sure, as she said! Oh Love, Love! even in death we shall not be parted. She will mourn over your cold clay; but your spirit will be with me, with me! You would have lived for her, but I die for you. Ah, God! how much sweeter death is, than life. Oh, my Love, my Love, you shall not take the journey alone! Whatever the great mystery is, we will solve it together. May Christ receive our spirits."

She emptied the powder into her sweetly-parted lips, folded the handkerchief under her cheek, and lay quite still, as if she slept.

When Lorette came in the morning, she found her lying in the same position, the handkerchief under her cheek, and a sweet, glad smile upon her dead face.

The papers, on the following day, reported the sudden death, by heart disease, of beautiful Madame Percy, a young French lady.

CHAPTER XXIII. BITTER SWEET.

In the afternoon of the next day, Homer Orton presented himself at Percy's apartments, only to be met by Mrs. Griffith, and informed of that young man's critical condition.

"He is slightly easier to-day," she said, "but we are instructed to keep him very quiet. There is little hope entertained of his recovery."

The journalist stood for a moment silent, shocked, bewildered. Then he spoke:

"I wish to consult him upon a matter of the gravest importance. Can you direct me to his most intimate friend or relative, to whom I might impart some very serious information? It is a matter which cannot wait."

Mrs. Griffith was impressed with the earnestness of the young man's manner. Reluctantly she stepped into the adjoining study, where Helena's shapely form lay stretched upon a broad lounge. It was the first respite she had taken from her position as watcher. She seemed to be sleeping, and Mrs. Griffith spoke her name softly, unwilling to disturb her.

But Helena was not sleeping. Though worn out with fatigue and excitement, the memory of Dolores' face, as it appeared for one brief, terrible second at the door of Percy's apartment, drove slumber from her pillow.

The consciousness that her old friend was in the city, near to her, suffering all the agonies of slighted wounded love, wrung her gentle heart with inexpressible pain. She longed to go to her, to take her in her arms, to comfort her. She longed to bring her to Percy's bed-side, and to say: "Stay here with me; together we will minister to his dying needs; it is our mutual right, our mutual sorrow." But even if she could find Dolores, that suffering tortured woman would turn from her, in bitterness and anger.

And Percy must not know that she was in the city; the knowledge might prove fatal to him in his weak, exhausted condition.

She arose wearily as Mrs. Griffith made known her errand.

"Do not let Percy know, that I am disturbed:" she said. "He made me promise to sleep until evening, without once leaving my couch. He would be annoyed if he knew I had disobeyed him."

"What! using authority so soon?" playfully asked Mrs. Griffith.

Helena answered only by a sad smile, as she passed out to meet Homer Orton. He arose with surprise, confusion, and distress mingled in his expression, as his eyes fell upon a comely young woman.

"I had a very painful piece of information to impart to Mr. Durand," he began, "and wished to ask his advice on the proper course to pursue. It is, however, a matter so extremely personal and of such a delicate nature, that I hardly know how to broach it to you. Are you a relative?"

"I am Mr. Durand's nearest friend and confidant. We are very closely related indeed," Helena answered quietly. "Please proceed with what you have to say."

Homer drew a copy of the morning paper from his pocket.

"This paper reports the sudden death of an acquaintance of Mr. Durand," he said. "We both knew her abroad; but it seems she has been living in New York under an assumed name, or at least under the name of Madame Percy. I recognized her this afternoon as I visited her remains in company with another journalist, as the lady who had bestowed most graceful hospitality upon both Mr. Durand and myself, while we were abroad. I feel personally interested in her as a friend, and I am certain, that he also does. Whatever her secrets, or her sorrows, I desire to keep them from the daily papers. I wished the advice and assistance of Mr. Durand in this matter. The apartments of the deceased lady are left in care of a French maid who cannot speak a word of English. Unless some friend takes charge of her effects, it will be impossible to avoid an exposure of what I fear is a painful history."

"Exposure must be avoided at any cost," cried Helena, her voice choked with tears, her heart torn anew over this additional and unexpected sorrow. "Madame Percy was a dear friend of mine. I know her entire history; it is most sad, most unfortunate, but it must not be given to the public; it must not be discussed by curious people who did not know her as I knew her, to love and to pity."

"It need not be given to the public," Homer Orton answered, firmly. "But you must go at once and take charge of her effects. The knowledge that she has friends in the city will prevent the sensation-seekers from ferreting out her history. You can give the reporters such facts as you choose concerning her life, if they approach you, and I will use my influence to prevent anything unpleasant from creeping into print."

And so, while Percy believed Helena to be sleeping, she performed the last sad rites for the woman who had been her dearest friend and her unintentional foe. With the exception of faithful Lorette, she was the only mourner to shed tears as the beautiful body was lowered to its last resting-place. Tears made more scalding and bitter by the thought of another burial drawing near, where she must officiate in the lasting character of a life-long mourner.

A story which closes with a suicide and a death is not a pleasant story to relate, or to read. Yet we who peruse our daily papers, know that such stories are very true to life.

It is gratifying to me, however, that I need not complete my narrative with a double tragedy.

Percy did not die.

It might have been owing to the mental condition produced by the knowledge that Helena was really his wife, or it might have been due to the skill of his physician; but certain it is, that he recovered, recovered, to realize that he had gained a wife almost by "false pretenses;" and that Dolores was no longer in existence upon the earth where she came an undesired child, and from which she went forth a suffering, desperate woman.

Shocked and almost crazed with the knowledge of this tragedy, Percy called Helena to him, a few hours after she had imparted the sad information.

"I feel like a cheat and a liar," he said; looking mournfully in her eyes, "to think I did not die as I promised. But I shall not offend you with my presence long. As soon as my strength permits I am going abroad, to remain an indefinite time. I feel that I shall never return to my native land; something tells me I shall find a grave among strangers. Our marriage will, of course, remain a secret with the few who know it now, and need cause you no annoyance."

Percy followed out the course of action he had set for himself, but, as is frequently the case with presentiments of evil, his impression that he was to find a grave among strangers was not verified.

He returned, after two years spent in travel, bronzed and robust, the light of his pure love for Helena shining more warmly than ever in his blue eyes.

It is so easy for a man to live down the errors that a woman (Christ pity her) can only expiate in the grave.

He reached out his arms, when he once more stood face to face with Helena.

"Can you not forgive all that miserable darkened past, and come and brighten the future for me?" he asked, in a voice that was like a caress. "I love you and I need you, Helena."

She looked up into his face, her eyes heavy with unshed tears. The love in her heart triumphed over every preconceived resolve, over every cruel, agonizing memory, as great love always must.

Yet there are triumphs sadder than any defeat: there are joys more painful than any woe. It was such a triumph, and such a joy, that filled Helena's heart as she glided into her lover's embrace.

"Oh, yes, I can forgive it all," she sighed. "Because I love you and because I am a woman. I sometimes think, Percy, that God must be a woman. He is expected to forgive so much."

Into her great heart, as she nestled upon his breast, in this supreme hour of reconciliation and recompense, there shot a keen, agonizing memory of the woman she had displaced; of the woman who had wrecked her whole happiness and lost her life in an unwise love for this man, whose tender, passionate words were falling now upon willing ears.

It was a memory which must, to a nature as generous and unselfish as hers, cast a melancholy shadow over the most intense hour of happiness the future could hold for her.

It was a phantom shape, which must sit forever at her feasts of love. Percy had made to her a complete surrender of his very soul; and she knew that their doubly wedded spirits, like two united streams, would mix and flow on together to the ocean of Eternity. Yet the more perfect her own joy, the deeper into her sympathetic heart must sink the sorrowful memories of Dolores.

Always, as she looked up to him with the worshiping eyes of a loyal wife, and saw in him her hero, her ideal, her protector and her guide, she must remember the young life his thoughtless, selfish folly helped to lay in ruins. All these emotions, robed the joy of that nuptial hour in mourning, as she lifted her sweet, sad face and filmy eyes to his.

And Percy, folding her in his arms, felt all a man's selfish pride, and all a lover's keen rapture in the knowledge that he was pressing the first kiss upon her pure lips, which had ever been placed there since her father's dying benediction fell upon them.

Ella Wheeler Wilcox – A Short Biography

Ella Wheeler was born on 5th November, 1850, on a farm in the village of Johnstown, Rock County, Wisconsin. Her parents, Marcus H. Wheeler and Sarah Pratt Wheeler, already had three children. A year earlier the family had moved from Vermont after Marcus's attempts at show business failed and becoming a farmer was his response. With Ella's birth they moved again. This time further north to Madison.

Ella was a gifted child, writing poetry and novels from an early age. The family was poor but her parents believed in education, and whilst little could be afforded they helped as best they could most usefully with grammar, spelling and vocabulary. Her initial education was at the local district school in the village of Windsor, now re-named in her honour as Ella Wheeler Wilcox School.

During her thirteenth year subscriptions the family had been receiving from the New York Mercury, a popular periodical, ceased. This greatly upset her. Life on the farm was lonely and the magazine had been a source of comfort and information about the big world beyond the farm. The family could not afford its own subscription so Ella had to make other plans.

Her writing ambitions were central to this. She wrote two essays but now had to obtain stamps so she could get her submissions in front of editors. She was corresponding with a young girl, Jean, who was in the freshman class at Madison University. Assuring her friend of future payment she enclosed the letter and essays for the New York Mercury.

By 1866, Jean, at Ella's behest, sent a list of all the monthlies and weeklies on the newsstands and Ella was hard at work saving pennies for postage as she began to mail them en masse with her works. Quickly her family lent their support to help out with her endeavours. Ella's mother especially had always thought her daughter would be the one to find the fame, travel and recognition that she had wanted herself and seeing the efforts Ella was putting in she was only to glad to help.

Soon the house the house was filled with ALL the periodicals. Editors would send magazines, books, pictures, bric-a-brac and tableware in response to Ella's requests and works. Being able to earn these items brought her great satisfaction and honed her skills.

She remembers the period in her autobiography:

"The very first verses I sent for publication were unmercifully "guyed" by my beloved "Mercury." The editor urged me to keep to prose and to avoid any further attempts at rhyme. He said that, while this criticism would wound me temporarily, it would eventually confer a favour on me and the world at large.

"My first check came from Frank Leslie's publishing house. I wrote asking for one of his periodicals to be sent to me in return for three little poems I had composed in one day. In reply came a check for ten dollars, saying I must select which one of some thirteen publications they issued at that time.

This bit of crisp paper opened a perfect floodgate of aspiration, inspiration and ambition for me. I had not thought of earning money so soon. I had expected to obtain only books, magazines and articles of use and beauty from the editor's prize-lists; and I had not supposed verses to be saleable. I wrote them because they came to me, but I expected to be a novelist like Mrs. Southworth and May Agens Fleming in time - that was the goal of my dreams. The check from Leslie was a revelation. I walked, talked, thought and dreamed in verse after that. A day which passed without a poem from my pen I considered lost and misused. Two each day was my idea of industry, and I once achieved eight. They sold, the majority, for three dollars or five dollars each. Sometimes I got ten dollars for a poem, that was always an event. Short love-stories, over which I laboured painfully, as story writing was an acquired habit, also added to my income, bringing me ten or fifteen dollars, and once in a while larger sums, from "Peterson's," "Demorest's," "Harper's Bazaar" and the "Chimney Corner."

Ella was beginning to understand the route to success and had the work ethic and creativity to turn it to her advantage. Ella would write her daily quota of poems and other works and then send them out to editors in the hope of getting them published.

It was also about this time that she also left the Country school. Her record in grammar, spelling, reading had of course been excellent but she had a horror of mathematics preferring to spend as much time as possible in the world of her imagination. Ella's talent and determination was such that by now, after she graduated from High School she was already well known in her state as a young writer.

In this she was encouraged by her mother, who despised her own life and felt herself and her family superior to all her neighbours and was forever impressing on the young teenager that her life would blossom and she would achieve success as a writer.

In 1867 her parents sent her to Madison where she was a junior in the Female College, a part of the University of Wisconsin. Ella wanted to spend all of her time writing and begged to come home. She didn't feel the need for further education and was painfully aware of the difference between her homemade clothes and the dresses of city girl. These and other differences caused her to feel left out and not part of the group. After many requests her parents relented and she was allowed home to continue her writing.

In 1870 she was offered employment at $45 a month to edit the literary department of a publication by the magazine's Milwaukee Editor. She accepted, but the hours and work were not to her liking and after three months the magazine folded and her single experience of working in an office was over. Now she was to be a full time author.

In 1872 she published her first book. It was an unusual step as it was a book of poems entitled 'Drops Of Water: Poems' that were solely about abstinence. Published by the National Temperance society it reflected her views on the evils of alcohol and earned her a $50 fee.

She published further books over the next decade but it wasn't until 1883 and the rather racy, for those times, publication of Poems of Passion that her success moved suddenly forward. It was an immediate and large scale success selling over 60,000 in two years.

That same year was also noteworthy for she was engaged to be married. Robert Wilcox was one of many suitors to the young Ella. He was a silver salesman from Meriden, Connecticut. Although they only met three times before the wedding it was to be the relationship that defined her life and much of her work. They married the following year in 1884.

Her most famous poem, "Solitude", was first published on 25th February, 1883 in an issue of The New York Sun. The inspiration for the poem came as she was travelling to attend the State Governor's inaugural ball in Madison, Wisconsin. Whilst travelling to the celebration she was sitting next to a young woman, dressed in black, who was in obvious distress. Ella comforted her for the whole journey. Recalling the widow's emotional state Ella wrote:

Laugh, and the world laughs with you;
Weep, and you weep alone.
For the sad old earth must borrow its mirth
But has trouble enough of its own

She sent the poem to the Sun and received $5 for her effort. It was collected in the book Poems of Passion shortly after in May 1883.

The newlyweds lived for a short time in Robert's home town of Meriden, Connecticut, before moving to New York City and then to Granite Bay in the Short Beach area of Branford, Connecticut. They built two homes and several cottages on Long Island Sound where they would hold gatherings of their literary and artistic friends.

On May 27, 1887, Ella gave birth to a son. Tragically he was only to survive for a few short hours.

In the early years of their marriage, they both developed an interest in theosophy, New Thought, and spiritualism. As this developed Robert and Ella Wheeler Wilcox promised each other that whoever died first would return and attempt to communicate with the other.

Ella had by now published many books of poetry as well as novels and other writings. Her writing life was filled with success on a national scale. Some volumes were collections based on a theme others on a particular time. Some of her war poetry that centred on the Great War in Europe is quite compelling. As she was never considered literary but rather mass market a lot of her work has not received the recognition that other lesser writers have obtained.

In 1916 after thirty years of marriage Robert Wilcox died. Ella was naturally devastated and desperate. Rather than dissipate her grief seemed to grow ever more intense as the days and weeks went by with no message from him. She journeyed to California to see the Rosicrucian astrologer, Max Heindel, seeking help in her sorrow as to why she had no word from Robert. She writes:

"In talking with Max Heindel, the leader of the Rosicrucian Philosophy in California, he made very clear to me the effect of intense grief. Mr.

Heindel assured me that I would come in touch with the spirit of my husband when I learned to control my sorrow. I replied that it seemed strange to me that an omnipotent God could not send a flash of his light into a suffering soul to bring its conviction when most needed. Did you ever stand beside a clear pool of water, asked Mr. Heindel, and see the trees and skies repeated therein? And did you ever cast a stone into that pool and see it clouded and turmoiled, so it gave no reflection? Yet the skies and trees were waiting above to be reflected when the waters grew calm. So God and your husband's spirit wait to show themselves to you when the turbulence of sorrow is quieted".

It seemed good advice. She wrote herself a short affirmative prayer to help calm her inner turmoil and would repeat it to herself over and over:

"I am the living witness: The dead live: And they speak through us and to us: And I am the voice that gives this glorious truth to the suffering world: I am ready, God: I am ready, Christ: I am ready, Robert."

She had already written in 1915 a booklet 'What I Know About New Thought which had sold over 50,000 copies. These and other books on New Thought, together with her expanding efforts to educate a wider audience to the powers of positive thinking, were a great comfort to her.

Ella expresses this unique blend of New Thought, Spiritualism and Reincarnation with these powerful words:

"As we think, act, and live here today, we built the structures of our homes in spirit realms after we leave earth, and we build karma for future lives, thousands of years to come, on this earth or other planets. Life will assume new dignity, and labour new interest for us, when we come to the knowledge that death is but a continuation of life and labour, in higher planes".

Ella fell ill in France in early 1919. It was breast cancer. She was taken initially to England and then back to her home. She died of the cancer on October 31, 1919.

Her final words in her autobiography 'The Worlds and I' were:

"From this mighty storehouse (of God, and the hierarchies of Spiritual Beings) we may gather wisdom and knowledge, and receive light and power, as we pass through this preparatory room of earth, which is only one of the innumerable mansions in our Father's house. Think on these things".

A Concise Bibliography

1872	Drops of water, poems.
1873	Shells.
1876	Maurine.
1883	Poems of Passion.
1886	Mal Moule'e, a novel.
1886	Perdita, and other stories.
1888	The Adventures of Miss Volney.
1888	Poems of Pleasure.
1891	A Double Life.
1891	How Salvator Won, and other recitations.
1892	Was it Suicide?
1892	The Beautiful Land of Nod.
1892	An Erring Woman's Love.
1892	Sweet Danger.
1893	The Song of the Sandwich.
1893	Men, Women and Emotions.
1896	An Ambitious Man.
1896	Custer, and other poems.
1897	Three Women.
1897	Roger Merritt's Crime.
1901	Every-day Thoughts in Prose and Verse.
1901	Poems of Power.
1902	The Heart of the New Thought.
1902	Kingdom of Love and How Salvator Won.
1902	The Other Woman's Husband.
1902	Poems of Life.
1904	Around the Year with Ella Wheeler Wilcox.
1904	A Woman of the World.
1905	Mizpah; or, the story of Esther, poetical drama in four acts.
1905	Poems of Love.
1905	Poems of Reflection.
1905	The Story of a literary career.
1906	Poems of Sentiment.
1906	New Thought pastels.
1906	Poems of Peace.
1907	The Kingdom of love, and other poems.
1907	The Love Sonnets of Abelard and Heloise.
1908	New Thought - common sense and what life means to me.
1908	Poems of Cheer.
1908	Selected Poems.
1909	Poems of Progress and New Thought Pastels.
1909	Sailing Sunny Seas.
1910	Diary of a Faithless Husband.
1910	The New Hawaiian Girl; a play.
1910	Poems of Experience.
1910	Yesterdays.
1911	Are you Alive?

1912   Picked Poems.
1912   Gems from Ella Wheeler Wilcox.
1912   The Englishman and other Poems.
1914   Poems of Problems.
1914   The art of Being Alive.
1914   Cameos.
1914   Lest we Forget.
1914   Poems of Ella Wheeler Wilcox.
1915   Poems of Optimism.
1916   World Voices.
1916   More Poems.
1916   Poems of Purpose.
1917   Poetical Works of Ella Wheeler Wilcox.
1918   Sonnets of Sorrow and Triumph.
1918   The Worlds and I.
1919   Poems.
1919   Cinema Poems and others.
1919   Hello Boys!

Published Posthumously
1920   Poems of Affection.
1920   Great Thoughts For Each Day's Life.
1924   Collected Poems of Ella Wheeler Wilcox.
1927   Gems from E.W.Wilcox

www.ingramcontent.com/pod-product-compliance
Lightning Source LLC
Chambersburg PA
CBHW071322130626
46556CB00004B/1701